Cricket and the Crackerbox Kid

Also by Alane Ferguson
SHOW ME THE EVIDENCE

Cricket and the Crackerbox Kid

by Alane Ferguson

BRADBURY PRESS
NEW YORK

Bradbury Press
An Affiliate of Macmillan, Inc.
866 Third Avenue, New York, NY 10022
Collier Macmillan Canada, Inc.
Printed and bound in the United States of America
First Edition
10   9   8   7   6   5   4   3   2   1
The text of this book is set in 12 point Baskerville.

Library of Congress Cataloging-in-Publication Data
Ferguson, Alane.
Cricket and the crackerbox kid/by Alane Ferguson.—1st ed.
p.   cm.
Summary: Pampered eleven-year-old rich kid Cricket thinks she has
finally found a friend in Dominic, who lives in the low-income
houses called crackerboxes, until they quarrel over ownership of a
dog and their classroom becomes a courtroom to decide who is right.
ISBN 0-02-734525-4
[1. Friendship—Fiction.   2. Dogs—Fiction.   3. Schools—Fiction.]   I. Title.
PZ7.F3547Cr   1990
[Fic]—dc20   89-39291   CIP   AC

*To Savannah Leigh Anderson and her
parents, Al and Maxine*

*As a stone leaves circles in a pond, the waves
of your love will reach out forever.*

1

"MONEY! WELL, THAT'S SOMETHING, ANYWAY."

Cricket Winslow pocketed the dime, then flipped another stone onto its back with the edge of her stick. She stooped to examine the cup-shaped depression the rock had left. Nothing. Just a dried sow bug clinging to a leaf. She flipped over another stone, then another. It was stupid, what she was doing. Eleven years old and looking for treasure underneath rocks and leaves. Babies did that kind of stuff—she was too old to pretend to be an explorer hunting the creek bed for gold. What if one of the kids from school saw her? Glancing around quickly, Cricket checked to see if anyone was watching, but the woods looked empty.

It was, after all, her property. The dried-up creek was technically hers; even the trees that stood like row upon row of gnarled skeletons belonged to her family. Two whole acres of property! And not a real friend to share them with.

Cricket stood and kicked leaves into the air. Their maid, Lois, had the day off, and her mom wouldn't be home until seven. "I hate Thursdays!" she complained aloud. "I hate being left alone!"

October wind rattled in reply, spinning fistfuls of the leaves to the ground. Holding out her palm, Cricket squinted at the clouds. Rain, maybe snow, was on the way. It was time to go. That's when she heard the sound.

Eeeooowwww!

It started low, then ended like a train whistle gone flat.

Somewhere, from deep in the underbrush, came that eerie, howling sound. Was it a ghost? Lois once told her spirits haunted this exact patch of earth, floating like cold mist over the treetops. Could it be. . . ? No, Cricket told herself fiercely, that was just a story. Lois was always making things up.

2

Oooooooooooooooooeeeeeeeeeeeeeeeeeeeee!

Her heart bounced against her ribs. Okay, she thought, don't be scared, just think it through. Halloween is five days away. Somebody's trying to spook you for a joke. Kids from school—yeah, that was it. It could be Ryan, or Heather and Melanie, or maybe even Skye. Peering into the dusk, she strained to find a flash of color or the top of a hat, but the shadows knit together to form an ominous black web. Even the rocks seemed to grin with eerie shadow faces.

Wwwwhhhhhhooooooooooooeeeeeeeee.

It wouldn't be Ryan or Heather or Skye, she realized as the moan snaked through the trees, because none of them liked her enough to play a trick. It was probably just some stupid Cracker-box kid from one of the little rectangular homes they called Crackerbox houses. When the school district boundaries were changed, half of Woodland Elementary ended up being Crackerbox. One of them was probably laughing at her, betting she'd run scared. Well, she'd show them!

"Whoever it is, get off my land!" she called out. "Do you hear me?" Trying to keep the waver from her voice, she yelled, *"I am not afraid!"*

Arp! Arp! Arp! Arp! Arp! Arp!

"Oh, for heaven's sake," Cricket cried, releas-

3

ing a breath she hadn't known she'd been holding. "It's a dog!" No one was trying to play a joke on her after all. Figured.

Pushing through the brush, Cricket followed the sound about a hundred yards, right to the edge of her land. And there, stuck in the middle of a mulberry bush, thrashed a black-and-white springer spaniel. It was a beautiful animal with a thick chest and a broad, almost squared face. Brown eyes, so wide the whites showed at the edges, followed Cricket's every motion. The barking turned to whimpering.

"Oh, you're stuck," she said gently. "Don't be scared—I'm a friend." Stretching out her hand, Cricket moved closer. She stopped inches away so the dog could get used to her scent.

"It's your collar, isn't it? Caught right on a branch. I bet I could get it off if you let me." Twigs popped as the dog shrank away from her, back into the brush.

"Don't do that," Cricket cried. "You'll get stuck worse!"

She squatted to eye level, then touched the dog's head lightly with her fingertips. "I'm Cricket. Well, I'm really Kristin, but my nickname is Cricket."

The dog shook again as Cricket stroked its

head. "There's no tag on your collar, and I can't just call you Dog. I know! How about if I call you Treasure? You're the best thing I've found all day."

The fur felt as smooth as glass against her palm. "You sure are a pretty girl. I always wanted a puppy, but, well, my mom says 'the best dog is a stuffed dog.' Now don't get nervous. I'm trying to help."

Slowly, hardly letting herself breathe, Cricket ran her hand down to the collar buckle. From reading books she knew that a dog's throat was its most vulnerable spot. A scared dog could give her a nasty bite.

"See, Treasure, this won't be hard. If I can just get . . . it . . . off!" Her fingers felt stiff as she pulled, then yanked until the buckle released and the dog wiggled free.

Barking, yelping, Treasure ran in tight circles, shook herself furiously, then zigzagged between trees and rocks, her nose pressed into the leaves as though she could suck the smells right into her mouth. Balls of black fur hung in clumps beneath her belly, like pom-poms on a lamp shade. Her coat bristled with burrs and dried leaves.

"Where are you going? As long as I saved you, we might as well do something. Can you fetch?"

As Treasure streaked after the stick, Cricket thought of her house and its large, polished rooms and soft gray carpet. Her mother always said their home wasn't the type where animals lived, but, Cricket decided, it wouldn't hurt for one to visit. How bad would it be to bring Treasure inside for just a little while?

"I bet you're hungry, aren't you?" Cricket asked. "And thirsty, too. You want a hot dog? I've got some at my house—they're gourmet."

Ignoring her, Treasure cocked her head at a bug skittering beneath the leaves. Cricket tried again. Slapping her thighs with her hands she called, "Food, Treasure. Ummhh . . . hot dogs from Germany—wieners!"

The dog focused warm eyes on her. Wind riffled the feathery hair on the backs of its legs.

"Come on, Treasure, just for a little while!"

The dog scanned the woods for the last time, searching the trees for something, someone, then bounded over to where Cricket stood.

"That's my girl! My Treasure!" Cricket cooed, rubbing behind her ears. "We'll eat dinner together, till my mom gets back. It'll be fun! Okay?"

Trotting obediently at Cricket's heels, Treasure followed her home.

"Mom, are you here?" Cricket called through the kitchen door. No answer. "Come on in, Treasure. She can't say I didn't try, right?"

Scurrying past her, Treasure wove through the kitchen, investigating the new smells of the Winslow house. She paused at the doorway to a bathroom, then darted inside. Seconds later Cricket heard the sound of water being lapped.

"What are you doing in there?" she asked, peering inside. "Oh, no! Not the toilet—don't drink from that! Lois would have a fit, and so would Mom! You can't do stuff like that," Cricket puffed as she pulled Treasure away, "or they won't let you stay, even for a little while. And I was thinking, well, I did find you, and if you want, maybe you could live here. I mean, you were on our property, right?"

Treasure sat on the floor and tipped her head, licking droplets of water from the ends of her whiskers.

"Come on, I'll get you a real drink."

Cricket's footsteps echoed against tile as she crossed to the cupboards to rummage for a pie tin. Shiny copper pots, the color of her hair, hung from the ceiling. The chrome faucets, the refrigerator door, the toaster, all were polished to a dazzle. Lois really knew how to make their kitchen

7

sparkle. Maybe, Cricket worried, Lois would tell her mother she wouldn't clean with a dog in the house. No, Lois went home to three cats of her own. She couldn't complain too much about one black-and-white dog at the Winslow house. It was Cricket's mother, as always, who would put her foot down. Who would refuse to even listen to the idea of having a pet.

"I'll *buy* you a stuffed dog. I saw one at the Bon that was incredibly lifelike," her mother had said the last time Cricket brought up the subject. "But I simply can't handle another body underfoot."

"But *Mom,*" she'd pleaded, "a stuffed animal is a toy; I need something *real.* Please, Mom! I'd take care of it. I promise."

Her mother had removed her glasses, then rubbed the red marks they made on the side of her nose.

"I know you believe that," she'd sighed, "but my answer is still no."

"But . . ."

"No dog, Cricket. Case closed."

Case closed. Those were two words Cricket heard a lot. Her mother was a lawyer, and whenever Cricket tried to argue with her, she felt as though she were on trial. Her mother always got the last two words. Case closed.

"I'd have better luck with my dad," she told Treasure, half out loud. "But he's in Japan right now. I think." Careful, so as not to spill any water, Cricket placed the pie tin on the floor.

"See," she went on, as though Treasure understood, "my dad's an airline pilot. He's gone a lot, but he says he likes dogs. As long as they're purebreds and not mutts." She scrutinized Treasure, then added, "You *are* a purebred, aren't you?"

Treasure sniffed the water indifferently, then stretched her legs in front as she pushed her bottom up into the air. Her toes made little spikes when she yawned, and her backside dropped to the floor with a thump.

"Well," Cricket giggled, "close enough." The kitchen brightened as a bolt of lightning cut the sky, followed by a loud clap of thunder. Treasure trotted to the french double doors and pressed her nose against the glass.

"Whatcha lookin' at, girl? Are you scared of the rain?" Cricket pulled a hot dog from the refrigerator and set it on the cutting board. "Don't be frightened. I used to get scared when it stormed, but it's different with you here. I mean, now we have each other." She sliced the hot dog into quarter-sized bites. "I've been thinking about something ever since I found you. You know what

9

it is, girl? I can tell you don't have anybody by the mess your coat's in. I mean, you're on your own, kinda like me. Don't get me wrong; I've got Mom and Dad, but . . ." She fed the hot dog slices to Treasure one at a time until they were gone, enjoying the soft, mooshy feel of the dog's mouth against her fingers. "If you stayed it would really be great. You could sleep on the floor in my room, and in the night, when it's dark, we could snuggle and . . . what is it, girl?" Cricket asked, looking up. "Why are you whining?"

Raising her paw, Treasure struck the door.

"You want to go outside? But it's raining."

Treasure scratched again, this time louder.

"Don't do that," Cricket cried. "You'll hurt the paint. Okay, if you've got to go, you've got to go. Just do it fast."

Fingers of rain slapped her face as Cricket opened the door. It was almost six-thirty. Dark clouds, as heavy and black as mountains, hovered above the ground. The grass was beaten smooth by the rain, and for a moment it seemed as though earth and sky were somehow reversed. Treasure darted onto the lawn.

"Hurry up, Treasure. I'm freezing!" Cricket called from the doorway.

Rain pelted the dog's coat, flattening it to her

10

body. Head high, Treasure sniffed the wind. She looked at Cricket, studied the woods, and then, with one long glance back, galloped into the darkness.

"Don't go so far," Cricket cried. "Come back, girl."

The white patch on Treasure's back dissolved to gray, then disappeared like a shadow joining the night.

"*No*!" Cricket screamed, "you're mine! *I found you*!" Tears mixed with the rain as she ran into her yard. Torrents stung her scalp, bit her skin, whipped through her clothes, but Cricket didn't care.

"Please," she called again, "come back!"

Suddenly lightning electrified the sky, and for an instant Cricket could see her whole yard. The lawn was empty. Treasure had vanished.

2

"ATTENTION, CLASS! ATTENTION!"

Mrs. Chumley clapped her hands together and pointed to the rules she'd listed on the chalkboard under the words How to Behave on a Field Trip. While the teacher talked, Cricket doodled a border around a picture she'd drawn. It was a pencil sketch of Treasure, and underneath she'd written Large Reward for Return of Dog. Of course she was just dreaming. Treasure had been gone for six days, and was certainly back home with her real owners. Cricket knew she'd never see the dog again.

"Rule number two," Mrs. Chumley went on. "Sit quietly on the bus. Field trips are a privilege; make sure you behave that way."

Slumping in her seat, Cricket stretched out her legs and tried to look bored. It wasn't that she was really truly bored, but it was important to look that way. It was a trick she'd learned a long time ago from—who had taught her that? Smiling, she remembered. It had been Whitney. Whitney Snow, her first and very best friend at Woodland Elementary School.

She'd been eight years old and one month into third grade when her parents moved to Pepperwood. Lois had driven her to Woodland on her very first day.

"Won't you take me inside?" Cricket had asked.

"Sorry, honey, I can't. Your parents told me to give you a big kiss, though." Awkwardly, she'd kissed the top of Cricket's head, then held her hand in a thumbs-up sign. "Good luck!"

Reluctantly, Cricket had gotten out of the car. She'd stood on the sidewalk, looking at the huge building and feeling very small. That's when she'd met Whitney.

"Hey, you're new here, aren't you?" Whitney had asked. Cricket turned to see a head of blond curls spilling from underneath a bright red ribbon, sharp blue eyes, and a cheek with a dimple in it.

"What's your name? I'm Whitney, and I'm in the second grade."

Whitney reminded Cricket of the "to-look-at-not-to-play-with" dolls her mother placed behind glass cabinet doors. Every part of her outfit matched, from her white tights with the tiny red hearts to her candy red earrings.

"Well. Don't you talk?" Whitney asked impatiently.

"My name is Cricket."

"Cricket!" Whitney snickered. "Why did your parents name you after a bug?"

Scraping the asphalt with the toe of her Reeboks, Cricket murmured, "I don't know. My real name's Kristin. But I like Cricket."

Whitney looked her over, up and down, and Cricket was glad she'd worn designer clothes. Her mother had picked every part of her outfit, right down to her socks, with special care. It somehow seemed to matter to Whitney. Swinging her red-and-white book bag onto her shoulder, she'd said, "I don't want to stand here anymore. I guess you can walk in with me."

Cricket hung back, afraid.

14

"Are you coming or what?"

Shaking her head no, Cricket hugged her sides. She felt as though she couldn't breath, as if her stomach were pinching her lungs.

Whitney had stood right in front of her and narrowed her eyes. She asked, "You're not scared, are you?"

Cricket looked away.

"Listen," Whitney had said, grabbing her arm. "You come with me."

She'd steered Cricket through the front doors of the school and pulled her into a small alcove. "I can tell you're not Crackerbox. You know, a kid from the yucky houses. So I'll tell you something," she went on in a solemn voice. "My brother—he's fourteen and super popular—told it to me." Leaning so close her curls brushed Cricket's cheek, she said, "You've for sure got to pretend like you're not afraid, even if you are. See, if you act scared, kids'll think you're a stupid baby. You won't get any friends."

She'd looked around, then put her pink lips right against Cricket's ear and whispered, "The other thing—this is the part that's sort of secret, so don't tell anyone—is you always got to act like you're the absolute best. My brother says if you do, everybody will believe it and you'll have con . . . con . . ." She rolled her blue eyes at the ceiling, searching for the word. The frown left her face as she cried, "Con-fi-dence! Get it?"

"But if I act like that, everyone will think I'm stuck-up."

Shrugging, Whitney had pulled away and said, "So?"

"I don't know." Cricket's voice was small.

"Well," Whitney had said, tossing her head, "I'll tell you one thing. It works for me!"

By the end of the year Whitney had moved away, but not before Cricket had learned everything she could about how to be popular. Now that she was in the fifth grade, pieces of advice still floated in her mind. To *be* cool, you have to *look* cool. Never act scared. Stay away from the Crackerbox kids.

She studied her fingernails as Mrs. Chumley chattered on.

"Rule number five: Remain together! The Animal Care and Control Facility does not want you wandering around. And last but not least, rule number six: Do not get too close to the cages. Remember, students," she said, underlining the words Show You Care: Be Aware!, "Animal Awareness Week means we have the opportunity to learn about pets and owner responsibility.

Now, get your buddies and line up!"

Cricket stood and watched the kids pair off.

"Stacey, can I ride with you?"

"How about it, Jeff?"

"Missy, you sit on one side and Candie can sit on the other."

No one rushed up to sit with Cricket. That was okay with her. Most of the kids in her class were dumb, anyway.

Just then Skye came bouncing over with Heather at her heels. "Cricket, why don't you go with Melanie? And hurry up, 'cause Mrs. Chumley says we can't save seats."

"I've just got to grab my sweater—" Cricket began, but Skye and Heather disappeared into the crowd at the doorway.

Shrugging, Cricket went to the coatrack, then turned to look for Melanie. The two of them usually paired off, but not because they were really great friends. It was just insurance against getting stuck with a Crackerbox kid or, even worse, a boy.

Cricket and Melanie boarded the bus second to last. All the good seats were already taken, so they slid into a green vinyl seat right behind the driver. Melanie got the window.

"I don't know why we have to go to a smelly pound," Melanie whined. "Do you know what happens to most of those animals? Do you? They're put to sleep. I don't want to see a lot of dogs on death row. It's sickening!"

Cricket dealt with Melanie the way she usually did. "Shut up, Melanie!"

"It's true. They take them in a gas chamber and *pssssss!*" Melanie clutched her throat and made gasping sounds.

"Don't be dumb. The dogs and cats get adopted. Mrs. Chumley said so."

"Do you always believe everything you hear? Most of those animals never get out, and I don't want to see one take the long walk." She popped her gum and asked, "Do you think animals go to heaven?"

Cricket sighed. "I think God made heaven *for* the animals, and I think *maybe* he'll let people in, *if* there's enough room. Now stop talking or you'll find out firsthand!"

Melanie giggled, then snapped a bubble between her teeth.

The Animal Care and Control Facility was a dingy building. A long, low rectangle capped with a flat tar roof, it seemed as gray and bleak as a prison. The walls were the type where cement oozed between the bricks, hanging down like globs of dried dough.

"Single file," Mrs. Chumley called in a loud voice. "Now, students, every single dog and cat in this building is up for adoption." She pointed toward the building and said, "Many beautiful animals are lost because their owners are careless, while others that end up here are simply abandoned. When an animal is picked up, here is where you'll find it. Let's go in, now."

There was shoving as the kids pushed through the entrance into the main office. A woman in a pink jumpsuit waved to them cheerily as they filed past her.

"Is everyone here?" Mrs. Chumley asked when they stopped at a door marked Adoption Center. "All right, stay together."

Yaps, barks, meows, every kind of noise an animal could make bounced off the cement walls and floor. It was dim inside, but Cricket could see cage after cage of animals. Cats and kittens paced in small cages; dogs of every kind pushed against the chain-link fence. The clamor was deafening.

"Ohhhh, it stinks in here!" Missy cried, holding her nose.

"Wow! It's *loud*!" Ryan bellowed.

"There are more than just dogs and cats!" Mrs. Chumley shouted over the din. "You can find such a variety—even birds! Look to your left, children. There's a boa constrictor!"

"Mrs. Chumley," Melanie called, looking from Cricket to her teacher. "How long do they keep the animals?"

An attendant stepped up to answer the question. His gray uniform matched the floor.

"My name is Bill Nichols, and I'd be happy to explain about our animal adoptions." He waved a stack of papers and smiled. "We keep every animal five working days. Anyone who wants to adopt simply fills out these forms, pays forty dollars, and takes home a new friend."

"What happens," Melanie yelled, "after the five days?"

Bill looked uncomfortable. He cleared his throat, then fingered the edge of his collar.

"We do the best we can. The real problem is lack of responsibility. If people would only spay and neuter their pets, there wouldn't be so many unwanted animals and we wouldn't have a problem."

"But what do you *do* with them?" Melanie insisted. Cricket remembered why she and Melanie weren't better friends.

20

"We . . . well, we hate to do it, but we have to put the animals to sleep."

Everyone groaned. Some of the kids shook their heads.

"It's not what we want to do," Bill protested. "Everyone here loves animals!"

"Murderer," Melanie mumbled.

Cricket broke away from the crowd. At least sixty dogs stood barking and clawing at the cages. Most were mixed breeds and a little scraggly, but to Cricket they were beautiful. Some of the bigger dogs, with their pointy noses and glowing yellow eyes, reminded her of wolves. The smaller dogs came in all types and colors: black curly fur on a poodle mix, terriers in every shade of brown. A dog with a crooked tail jumped over a puppy with egg-shaped spots. One dog had so much stringy hair it looked like a mop with legs. Holding her hand toward the cages, so they could smell her and not be afraid, Cricket walked on.

She glanced over her shoulder. Mrs. Chumley and Bill were holding the boa constrictor in the air. Its long body draped across their arms and swayed a foot above the floor. Some of the girls squealed nervously; Andy Smith darted his tongue in and out like a snake. No one noticed that Cricket had left the group.

Squatting on her heels, she let a salt-and-pepper cockapoo lick her hand. "You're cute!" she whispered. "I wonder if you shed on furniture?"

". . . skin is quite dry. Not slimy at all. Next, we'll go see the cats," Bill droned on.

Cricket looked over her shoulder and eyed her classmates nervously. She knew she wasn't supposed to be there with the dogs. If Mrs. Chumley caught her with her hand in the kennel, a note would go home for sure.

"Well, boy, I guess I'd better go." As she stood she caught sight of black-and-white fur. In a cage behind the cockapoos, curled up in the very corner, head pressed to the wall, lay a black-and-white dog.

Cricket's heart leaped. "Treasure?"

Her call excited the dogs even more, and they began to bark furiously. Everyone looked in Cricket's direction, but she didn't care. She called again, louder. "Treasure! Is that you?"

"Cricket, for heaven's sake! You know the rules," Mrs. Chumley cried. "Get back here!"

Cricket stood on her toes and strained to see. "Treasure! It's me, Cricket!" Suddenly Cricket felt a hand on her arm. It was Bill.

"I'm afraid you've got to come away from here.

It's barely possible an excited dog might scratch you through the chain-link—"

"No!" Cricket jerked her arm free.

"Miss!" Bill's voice grew louder. "You've got to move. Now!" He put both hands on her shoulders, but Cricket shrugged them off. Her fingers gripped the wire as she tried to see past the dogs that popped up and down like the figures in an arcade game.

"Mrs. Chumley!" Bill yelled.

Slowly, the dog raised its head, pulling itself up on its two front legs. Its hind leg dragged behind, taped in gauze. Cricket strained on tiptoe. She couldn't tell—couldn't see.

"Are you looking at the springer?" Bill finally asked. "Do you know that animal?"

Cricket stared at the shivering dog, at the grimy, snarled fur. She could barely get the words to move past her lips, until finally she cried, "I . . . yes! Yes! That's *my* dog!"

3

"*I* want her!"

"*Well, I don't!*"

Cricket felt her cheeks flame. "She's mine! I found her on our property!"

Between gritted teeth her mother replied, "That's like saying we own every person who happens to stand on our grass. Your argument is ridiculous!"

Cricket and her parents were seated in the living room. Snow fell outside in thick, heavy clumps. A fire burned on their gas log, casting golden lights across the walls but giving no warmth. Sitting stiffly on the embroidered couch, her mother crossed her legs and pulled her arms to her chest.

Cricket's father didn't look at her at all. He was busy picking a piece of lint off his forest green jogging suit.

"She's hurt!"

"She'll *shed*!"

"I don't want a mongrel," her father broke in, finally looking up.

"Treasure's no mutt, Dad; she's a purebred springer spaniel." Cricket bit the edge of her lip, then leaned toward her father, pleading. "Treasure's five days at the pound are up tomorrow! No one has taken her because she's hurt, and now they're going to kill her!"

Calm, almost wistful, her father said, "A child can learn a lot from an animal."

"Don't you dare make me the villain, Clifford," her mother warned. "You don't want a dog in this house any more than I do."

Cricket shrank into the couch as her parents glared at each other. It was one of those rare times when her father was home. Tall and thin, with dark, neatly trimmed hair and manicured hands, he smelled of breath mints and Aramis soap.

Pursing her lips, her mother continued. "May I

25

point out that this dog is injured? Who is going to take it to the vet? Hmmm? And who, might I ask, will clean the springer surprises from our lawn? Ever step in one of those?"

"I will!" Cricket cried. "I promise!"

Her father cleared his throat. "I'm just saying that the responsibility might do her good. . . ."

"Do her good! Remember the goldfish? A fish actually *drowned* because Cricket never cleaned the water in the bowl."

"But I was only six years old!" Cricket wailed.

"All right then, last year you demanded a piano. As I recall, you gave a solemn oath that you'd practice every single day, which you did for exactly three weeks . . ."

"Mom—"

". . . after which I had to practically beg you to play!"

"Now, Susan," her father protested. "We're discussing the dog, not the piano."

"One has everything to do with the other!" she snapped. "We're discussing commitment, reliability, and integrity. And I don't want to argue about this!" Her mother yanked her fingers through her hair. It was the color of brass, straight and smooth, with tiny streaks of gray. Her brown eyes could narrow in a way that made everyone

26

shut up. She could even scare a judge. But to-night, Cricket couldn't let herself get beaten down. She had to win for Treasure. It was life or death.

"Mom, I have something to say."

Cricket stood and began to pace. She had seen her mother pace that way in the courtroom, when she'd given closing arguments to a jury.

"I know that sometimes I haven't kept my promises—"

"That's exactly my point," her mother broke in.

"No! Let me finish! See, this is different. Treasure's like a friend. She's someone I could do things with, someone I could be with after school." Cricket faltered, "I . . . I hate being alone."

"Forget it, Cricket," her mother said calmly. "Your strategy won't work. What I hear you saying is that because I'm gone, you're lonely and therefore I owe you a dog. Well, I will not feel guilty for having a career, and I will not let you push me into getting an animal I don't want."

Cricket stopped pacing.

"Please," she began, her words clutched in her throat. "Don't do that, Mom."

Sometimes it was so hard to talk to her mother, and she wanted Treasure so much. It seemed

27

she'd never have the right words, words that were good enough, that could make her parents know how important this was. A ball of frustration grew inside her, squeezing out in tears.

"Cricket, why? Don't cry. Sweetheart, don't cry."

"B-b-but, I . . ."

"Come here. Sit down with us." Her father's strong arms pulled her down, sandwiching her between the two of them. They felt warm, and strong. Her mother rubbed her hair.

"You said 'don't do that.' What don't you want me to do?" Coaxing, her mother pressed, "You can tell me."

"It's just . . ." Cricket groped for the words. "Every time I try and talk, it's like, well, you . . ."

Placing her finger under Cricket's chin, her mother raised her face and stared into it.

"Tell me. What do I do?"

Cricket drew in a breath. How could she explain with those eyes boring into hers? Then she thought of Treasure and her wide, scared eyes. It gave her courage.

"You . . . you always win. Always."

Her mother dropped her hand. "I don't see what's wrong with that. . . ."

"But you win because you talk better." Cricket hesitated, then said, "Not because you're right."

Some of the fire went out in her mother's eyes. She seemed to sag, just a little.

"The child's right, Susan," her father added gently. "We poor mortals hardly have a chance."

"Do you feel that way too, Cliff?"

"Only when I want something as badly as Cricket does."

The grandfather clock struck nine, and the last chime lingered in the room like the sound of a plucked guitar string.

Finally, her mother straightened.

"If I step into anything, it's your hide!"

"You mean it?" Cricket hardly dared believe what she'd heard. "Really? I can have her? You truly mean it?"

"Yes, I mean it." Her mother smiled. "You have a very convincing case, Cricket. And wonderful assistance from your father. Honestly, Cliff, am I that bad?"

Her father laughed and nodded his head.

Springing out of the sofa, Cricket hugged her mother, then her father, as hard as she could. She'd won! The most important battle of her life, and she'd won.

Treasure was coming home.

4

CRICKET WOKE UP FEELING HOT. SHE TRIED TO stretch her legs, the way she did every morning, but she couldn't. Drawing her knees to her chest, she pushed with her feet as hard as she could. Treasure moaned and rolled on her side.

"Treasure, what are you doing up here! Mom'll kill me. And you!"

Treasure didn't look impressed. She gave a wide yawn; her pink tongue curled at the edges.

"Ooph . . . you're heavy . . . get down! Go on, get in your basket," Cricket puffed, pushing at Treasure's backside. She couldn't budge her.

Treasure lazily licked her paw. Her back leg, scraped and bruised, lay at a right angle to her body. Bill had explained that Treasure had been hit by a car, then brought to the pound because she hadn't had a license. It was lucky, he'd said, that Cricket had taken her. Most injured dogs never made it out.

"You know what you are?" Cricket asked as she stroked the velvety fur under Treasure's chin. "You're a stinker dog. I thought you'd be more like Lassie, but you're just about the stubbornest thing I've ever seen. I think I should have named you Trouble instead of Treasure." She stopped pushing Treasure's bottom and hugged her instead. Little sparks of static made a crackling sound as she rubbed her dog's back.

What Cricket said to Treasure was true. Having a dog wasn't at all the way she'd thought it would be. In her mind, she'd pictured Treasure fetching the morning paper, instantly obeying her every command. But this dog didn't follow instructions. No matter what Cricket said, or yelled, Treasure did exactly as she pleased.

The first day she'd brought her home Cricket had found Treasure curled on her mother's velvet chair. "No, Treasure, no!" she'd yelled. "Get off!"

Ten minutes later she'd discovered Treasure asleep on the same chair, drooling into burgundy velvet tucks.

"Oh, Treasure!" she'd sighed. "You are a pain!"

And now, even after a whole week of training, Treasure still drank right out of the toilet. She stole sandwiches from the counter and had chewed a hole in her father's sock.

But in every other way, having Treasure was better than Cricket could have imagined. From the moment Cricket opened her front door after school to the time she closed her eyes at night, she and Treasure stayed together. They were best friends.

"You know what I like about you?" Cricket asked as she kissed the patch of fur above Treasure's nose. "You're the absolute best listener. Like when I tell you stuff, you never say, 'Do you know what your problem is?' Nope, you just lick my hand and . . ."

Suddenly, Cricket heard her mother's voice echoing in the hallway. She was talking to Lois, and they were heading toward her room.

"Oh, no. Off, Treasure! Please!"

"Cricket, are you up? You're going to be late for school."

32

"I'm up, no need to come in. . . ."

"But I want a kiss good-bye!"

The footsteps grew closer as Cricket gave Treasure another desperate shove. She didn't budge. Grabbing the corner of her comforter, she threw the entire cover over Treasure, hiding everything but the black tip of her nose.

The bedroom door swung open.

"You're still in bed, sleepyhead. I've got another late night, so I thought I'd— Where's Treasure?"

Cricket gulped. "Treasure? She's . . . uh, she's . . ."

Her mother's hands flew to her hips.

"She's on your bed again. I see her beady little eyes."

Treasure's nose had lifted the corner of the comforter. Cricket quickly pushed it down.

"That comforter cost two hundred and fifty dollars. It used to be white. Now you could stuff a pillow with the hair she's left on it!"

"I'm sorry, Mom. Treasure is so stubborn. I can't keep watch all night. She just sort of sneaks up."

"I could insist she sleep outside—"

"But *Mom!*"

"However, it *is* cold." Pausing, she studied

Cricket's pleading face. "You really love that dog, don't you?"

Cricket nodded as hard as she could. She watched her mother's mouth soften into a tiny smile; as she walked toward the bed, Cricket heard the slip-slip-slip sound of wool against silk and smelled the sweet scent of Eternity perfume. Perching on the edge of the bed, she smoothed her fingers over Cricket's tousled hair.

"I have a suggestion."

"What?" Cricket asked, biting her lip in anticipation.

"Why don't we put a large beach towel on your bed, and then—just give up?" She shook her head, grinned, and added, "That dog!"

"A towel! That's a great idea! Thanks, Mom!" It was hard to believe her mother could tolerate all the mischief Treasure got into. But she did. Somehow. Parents were certainly hard to figure.

Leapfrogging over Treasure, Cricket hugged her mother hard. "And I'll try and brush her more. That'll for sure help."

"Good! Then I think we've reached a solution beneficial to all parties—especially Treasure! Now hurry and move your own little tail or you'll be late for school!"

After her mother had gone, Cricket gave Treasure a final squeeze. "Go ahead and snooze, 'cause I know you've got to save your energy for eating and sleeping. Just remember, we'll be together the absolute second I'm back."

The dog sighed with contentment, and Cricket gave her one more kiss, then got up to dress for school.

The bell rang just as Cricket slid into her seat. Everyone in her class cut it as close as she did, scrambling into their chairs at the last possible second. Mrs. Chumley stood at the front of the room. A dark-haired boy stood quietly at her side.

"Settle down, class," she said, rapping a ruler on her desk. "People, I need your attention."

The noise died down. Everyone stared at the new boy. He was dressed like a kid from a Crackerbox house. Faded red and blue stripes ran across his knit shirt, his jeans were a half inch too short, and his running shoes looked crumpled. The boy stared at the back of the room, then at the floor. Cricket couldn't help but notice how scared he looked.

"This is Dominic Falcone. He just moved here from Florida. I'm sure he's not used to all this snow. Have you ever seen snow before, Dominic?"

Dominic cleared his throat. His face turned red. He didn't say a word.

"Have you seen snow, Dominic?" Mrs. Chumley pressed. She smiled encouragingly, but Dominic didn't look at her. He didn't look at anyone. Just the floor. Finally he muttered, "I've seen it."

"I bet his nickname is Dummy," Melanie snickered. The class giggled. Dominic flushed.

"What did you say, Melanie?" Mrs. Chumley asked.

"Nothing."

"Then don't speak out of turn. Let's all join together in welcoming Dominic to Woodland Elementary. Give Dominic a great big hello!"

"Hello," the class mumbled.

Cricket knew Dominic was already in trouble. Woodland sized up the new kids pretty fast, and Dominic had failed.

Even though over half the school was Crackerbox, he wouldn't fit in with them if he couldn't talk. And the Pepperwood kids for sure wouldn't take him. Once Cricket heard Skye and Heather make a secret list of the best way to tell a Crackerbox kid.

"The first thing is they always bring their own lunch," Skye had whispered.

"And at recess, they don't even care if they get messed up," Heather had added.

"And like, have you ever seen the way the girls wear their nail polish? Chipped!"

"Plus, Crackerbox always look like their mom cut their hair."

"Some are okay, I guess," Skye had offered, "but, I don't know. . . ."

Giggling, Heather had said, "At least they make us look extra good—standing next to them!"

Because she was Pepperwood, Cricket was sort of in their group, but she didn't like any of them much. And the Crackerbox kids seemed to stay away from her as much as she did them.

"Did you get all your books from the principal's office?" Mrs. Chumley asked the new boy now.

Dominic colored and nodded.

This kid is hopeless, Cricket thought. His clothes were wrong, he blushed, and he couldn't seem to talk. What a dud.

"You'll be sitting next to Kristin Winslow. We call her Cricket. You may take your seat, Dominic."

Cricket's heart sank. She looked at the empty seat on her right.

As Dominic walked down the aisle, Cricket

studied her desk top. Better not be too friendly or you'll get stuck answering stupid questions all day, she told herself. From under lowered lids she watched his shoes stop, hesitating by the desk.

"Yes, that's your seat," Mrs. Chumley said. "Now class, take out a clean sheet of paper. We're going to have a pop quiz on our spelling words."

Everyone groaned, including Cricket. This past week she'd been so busy with Treasure that she'd really slipped in her study habits.

"The first word is *dictionary,*" Mrs. Chumley began.

When the test was over, Mrs. Chumley asked the students to pass their papers to the left. Dominic looked at Cricket, then scribbled on his paper. He tossed his test over to Cricket.

Cricket didn't look, but as Dominic leaned toward her she smelled him. He smelled clean and fresh, like he'd been dipped in Irish Spring soap.

"The first word is spelled D-I-C-T-I-O-N-A-R-Y."

Dominic's handwriting was small and neat. Every one of his letters, even the *O*'s, looked square. Cricket glanced to the bottom of the page, then drew in a sharp breath. Scrawled in the bottom, in the very corner, was a message. And that message made her very angry.

5

CRICKET STARED AT THE WORDS DOMINIC HAD scrawled across his test. He wrote, "Is everyone at Woodland as snotty as you?"

If she hadn't had to pass it back, Cricket would have crumpled up his test and tossed it away. Who did he think he was, anyway? He'd been at Woodland all of five minutes and he was writing horrid things for her to read.

"*Character* is spelled C-H-A-R-A-C-T-E-R."

Cricket hoped Dominic would flunk, so she could mark his paper with angry red *X*'s, but he got every one right.

"Please return the papers to their owners," said Mrs. Chumley.

Cricket glared at Dominic, but he was busy handing Melanie her paper. In a flash she grabbed her pencil and wrote a message to him. It said, "Is everyone from Florida as stupid as you?"

Smiling sweetly, she gave Dominic his paper.

When he read what Cricket scribbled, the edges of Dominic's ears turned crimson. He grabbed a tablet of paper, tore off a piece, and scrawled another message. Then he folded the paper smaller and smaller, until he couldn't fold it anymore. When Mrs. Chumley turned her back, he tossed it over onto Cricket's desk. It said, "Did your parents name you Cricket 'cause you bug them? Or was it your buggy eyes?"

Cricket peeled a sheet of paper and wrote, "Don't your ankles get cold wearing pants that short?"

This time, when Dominic read his message, Cricket thought he almost smiled. It *was* kind of funny. What a strange boy this was. Here he couldn't say a word in front of the class, but could write a note faster than any girl she knew.

" . . . math assignment. Turn to page 106," Mrs. Chumley said. Cricket whipped out her book.

40

She'd better start paying attention. She was just getting to problem number nine when another small square landed right in the center of her book. Slowly, Cricket unfolded the tiny piece of paper. It said, "Where do you live? Just so I don't walk that way."

She stared at the note, then shot a look at Dominic, but he was engrossed in his math. Even though he wrote "just so I don't walk that way," Cricket sensed he wanted to be friends. With her. There wasn't a girl she considered a true friend, much less a boy. She studied him again, keeping her eyes down so no one could tell she was looking. His brown hair was cut short and his nose was small and straight; from the side Cricket could tell his lashes were bristly black and longer than hers. He was just a tiny bit cute. She thought back to her first day at Woodland. Maybe she could tolerate him, just a little. She decided to write one more message. "Dominic, I live in Pepperwood. I've got a new dog named Treasure. Do you have a dog?"

That's when it happened. A large hand, Mrs. Chumley's hand, swooped onto Cricket's desk and grabbed the note.

"I see you're busy with something other than your math, Cricket. You know the rules. Any notes that I catch are read out loud to the class."

"Oh, no, that's my . . ." Cricket cried, but it was too late.

" 'Dominic,' " Mrs. Chumley read. " 'I live in Pepperwood.' "

"Oooooohhh," whistled some boys. Cricket felt her face burn.

Mrs. Chumley glanced over the rest of the note, then returned it to Cricket. She didn't want to embarrass her any more.

"You all know passing notes during class is forbidden. But I think it's nice that Cricket is trying to make Dominic feel at home."

Melanie made some kissing sounds in her hand. The class giggled.

"Now let's get back to work."

Cricket could hardly see the pages in her book, she was so embarrassed. It was bad enough to get caught writing notes. It was humiliating to have it read. But she'd had the worst, the absolute worst thing happen to her. She was caught writing a note to a boy!

Mrs. Chumley walked back up the aisle and stopped right between Cricket and Dominic. She squatted so her eyes were level with theirs.

"Cricket, Dominic," she whispered. Even

though she spoke softly, Cricket was positive the rest of the class could hear.

"I've been concerned about the science project I assigned yesterday. Everyone has a partner except Cricket. So what I'd like to do, instead of either one of you doing a project alone, is give you an assignment to do together. Is that okay with you? Dominic?"

Cricket could see Dominic nod his head. He looked like he would melt through the floor.

"Cricket?"

Cricket's heart was pounding so hard she could barely hear. What could she say? No? To her teacher! And after Dominic had said it was all right? Then *she'd* be the one to get in trouble.

"Cricket?"

"Sure. Fine," Cricket finally mumbled under her breath.

Mrs. Chumley smiled, then stood up. Her knees creaked.

"Good. See me after school. I'll fill Dominic in and give you your assignment."

As Mrs. Chumley walked away, Cricket tore Dominic's note into tiny pieces. Now she'd be late getting home to Treasure, and she was stuck with Dominic on a project. Not only that, but the whole class probably thought she was in love. Whoever heard of a boy writing notes? A boy from Florida with stupid-looking shoes. Darn him, anyway!

6

THE CLASSROOM HAD ALMOST EMPTIED BEFORE Cricket walked in. Ryan Jones and Michael Bower were feeding gerbils on a counter behind the teacher's desk. Mrs. Chumley frowned in concentration as she recorded test scores in a black spiral notebook. Dominic was nowhere in sight.

"Oh, hello, Cricket," Mrs. Chumley said, looking up. "Come on in. Is Dominic with you?"

At the sound of Dominic's name, Ryan rolled his eyes at the ceiling and batted his lashes like moth wings.

"No," Cricket muttered.

"Well, then, while we're waiting I'd like to say

how proud I am of you, Cricket. Not for passing notes, of course, but for being so friendly. Being the new kid is hard. I think you've made Dominic's first day a lot easier."

Michael puckered his lips and beat his hand over his heart. Ryan stuck his finger down his throat as though he were gagging.

Without turning around, Mrs. Chumley asked, "Michael, Ryan, how would you like to do an assignment on manure—one that includes samples?"

The boys looked at each other, then quickly ducked out of the room, leaving Cricket alone with Mrs. Chumley.

Leaning over her desk, the teacher clasped her hands to her chin and said, "Listen, Cricket, I know working with a boy is, well, unusual. But they *are* people. For the most part. Won't you try to be a good sport about this?"

Cricket didn't know what to say. She'd been all set to be sullen, to let Dominic know she hated being stuck with him. And now her teacher was talking to her like an equal. Like a friend. Sighing, she said, "Okay Mrs. Chumley, I'll try."

At that moment Dominic arrived, his backpack flung over his shoulder so that he seemed to droop on one side. His face was red again.

"Hello, Dominic," Mrs. Chumley said brightly. "I know it probably seems mean to give you homework on your first day, but I only made the assignment yesterday. You won't be behind the others."

Dominic stopped three feet from Cricket and stood so straight he looked stiff.

"The unit we are on is the study of mammals. You can do a report on any warm-blooded creature that hasn't been picked by someone else. Let me give you some examples of animals other children have signed up for."

Mrs. Chumley ran a chubby finger down her list. "Let's see, there's one on bears, and coyotes, and here's one on whales. Is there any animal you're particularly interested in, Dominic?"

Dominic shifted from foot to foot. He bit the edge of his lip.

"Do you want to see the list? Maybe that'll help you decide on something."

"I'd like to do a report on dogs."

Those were the first unmumbled words Cricket had heard Dominic say. His voice was clear and slightly deep for a boy in fifth grade.

"Dogs. Hmmm . . . I don't see dogs written

down. Is that okay with you, Cricket?"

Cricket's heart jumped. Dogs! A whole report on dogs—what a great idea! Had he picked that because of the note about Treasure? No, Mrs. Chumley hadn't read that part out loud. He must love dogs the way she did.

"I'd like to do that, too," Cricket said. Dominic finally looked at her. He smiled. His teeth were white.

"Good," Mrs. Chumley said. "You have four weeks to make your presentation. Good luck!"

Dominic walked beside Cricket until they pushed through the doors of Woodland Elementary. He was quiet, and Cricket had the feeling that he was watching her.

"Do you know what time it is?" Cricket asked, glancing around for a wall clock.

"I don't have a watch, but I think it's about twenty after three."

"Uh-oh, I think I'm going to catch it. Lois hates it when I'm late. And there she is."

In the family's silver Mercedes sat a fortyish woman in a navy blue jogging suit. Even from twenty feet away her face looked sullen.

Surprised, Dominic asked, "You call your mother Lois?"

"No, Lois is our maid."

"Oh." He paused for a minute. Cricket could tell he wanted to say something. She wished he'd hurry up.

"Um, Cricket?"

"Yeah?" Cricket held up her index finger to Lois, signaling one more minute. Lois drummed her fingernails against the steering wheel.

"I think I'd better get your phone number. So I can call you about the report."

"Sure." Cricket opened her notebook and wrote her number.

"Would you like to come over to my house right now? I mean, so we can get a head start." His words came out rushed, as though one word pushed the next from his mouth.

"I can't," Cricket said. "I've got to take care of my dog. She's waiting for me."

Dominic looked at the ground, then at a clump of trees to his right.

"No problem. I just don't want to get a bad grade."

Cricket could tell Dominic was embarrassed. His ears were getting red again. Or maybe it was the cold.

"See ya, Cricket."

"Yeah. See ya tomorrow."

"Hey, do you want a ride?" Cricket asked suddenly. "We can take you home."

Dominic studied the Mercedes.

"No thanks."

As Lois pulled away from the curb, Cricket watched Dominic walk down the street. He hunched a little when he walked, probably to keep the wind from biting his skin. Like his jeans, his jacket was a size too small. Cricket pictured an afternoon with Dominic, munching some popcorn while they browsed through books on dogs. Maybe they could play a few games together. They could talk about school, and she could fill him in on which kids to avoid at all costs. But, Cricket reminded herself, Treasure would be waiting.

Later, when they pulled into her driveway, Cricket saw Treasure's face disappear from the window and heard frantic barking behind their front door.

"I'm here, Treasure, I'm back now!" Cricket cried as she ran inside. Treasure wagged her tail so hard her whole body danced with excitement. Dropping to her knees and pulling her close, Cricket breathed in Treasure's sweet doggie smell. I'm home, she thought. With my dog. And she's the only friend that matters.

50

7

"I'M GOING TO GET MY HAIR PERMED FOR THANKS-
giving," Skye announced as she cut a piece of
soggy turkey on her lunch tray.

"Really!" Melanie squealed. "How are you
going to do it? Tight or loose?"

It was one of those days when Cricket tagged
along with Melanie. Even though she was invited,
Skye and Heather made her feel as though including her was pure charity.

"I'm going to get it done in big, loopy curls,"
Skye answered, twisting a piece of smooth blond
hair.

51

"Ooohh, that sounds cool. Are you getting it cut, too?" Heather asked.

"No. Just a perm."

"Well," Cricket said, leaning into the table so they could all see her, "be careful you get it done right. You for sure don't want your hair to look worse than it does right now."

"What's that supposed to mean?" Skye asked. Cricket didn't notice her eyes flashing.

"I just meant fuzzy poodle hair looks a lot worse than straight hair. The lady at my mom's salon never lets it frizz—"

"What's wrong with straight hair?" Heather broke in. "That's real nice, Cricket. You just told Skye her hair's ugly."

Coloring, Cricket snapped, "No, I did not."

"Yes you did! You said, 'Skye, you don't want your hair to look any worse than it already does'!"

"I didn't either."

"Uh-huh. Didn't she, Melanie?"

As Melanie nodded, Cricket quickly said, "If I did, that's not what I meant. What I *meant* was . . ."

But Skye wasn't listening. She grabbed her tray and stood up. "You know, you'd have a zillion more friends if you'd just learn to shut up! Come on, guys!"

"Nice going, Cricket!" Melanie hissed as she swung her legs over the bench.

"But I'm not done eating!" Heather complained.

"Fine!" Skye snapped. "You can sit with The Mouth by yourself."

Heather took a big bite of turkey and shoved a roll in her pocket. "Wait! I'm coming!" The three of them flounced off, leaving Cricket alone with her half-eaten food.

Why did that always happen? Cricket wondered. She didn't mean to say the wrong things, but somehow her words seemed to get turned around. Maybe it was because she was an only child. That's what she'd heard her mother whisper one night. "Cricket has never learned to interact. She's had too many adults in her life."

"Can't we hire a friend for her?"

"Cliff!"

"I was only kidding. Cricket's a great kid. She'll learn."

But she'd never been able to figure out the secret. Following Whitney's advice made her seem like a snob, and the real true snobs like Skye

53

didn't like her a bit. At least I have Treasure, she thought to herself fiercely.

She took another mouthful of potatoes. They tasted like straw.

"How ya doin', Cricket?"

Looking around quickly, Cricket saw Dominic standing with a lunchbox in his hand. It had a picture of a California Raisin on it.

"I'm okay, I guess."

By then most of the kids were on their way out of the lunchroom. She checked to see if anyone was watching them, but no one was. She didn't want to be teased about being in love again.

Banging his lunchbox against his thigh, Dominic said, "Yeah, well, I was just thinking how we need to get together and work on our report. Is it okay if I sit here a second?" He flushed a little, but not as much as on the first day.

"Sure. The table's empty."

Slipping beside her, he asked, "So, when do you want to get started?"

"I don't know. It's not due 'til December seventh. That's three weeks away."

"Well, like I said, I hate to do stuff at the last second."

Today Dominic had on a green velour pullover

with rubbed out elbows. He'd forgotten to wear a belt, and part of his hair stood up at the top like tiny feathers. Still, Cricket thought, he looked nice.

Waving his hand toward Heather's disappearing back, he asked, "Are you and those guys friends?"

"Sort of."

"Hmmm."

Cricket searched for something to say. It was awkward talking to him, but better, she decided, than sitting alone. She finally settled on, "So, how do you like it here?"

She took a bite of corn and chewed slowly. With her mouth full, he'd have to do the talking.

"Woodland's all right. Most everyone is nice, but some of the kids are sorta stuck-up." Now he paused. He plucked at a thread on the cuff of his shirt. Suddenly he looked up and said, "You have a dog, right? What's he like?"

"Treasure?" Cricket asked, swallowing quickly. "Oh, she's great. I'm having so much fun with her. She's big . . . well, more medium-sized, and she takes up almost all of my bed at night. And when my dog barks you can really hear it. She's not one of those dumb little squeaker dogs that goes 'yip yip yip'—" Suddenly Cricket cringed. What if Dominic had a tiny dog? But he just looked at her and laughed.

"I know just the kind you mean. Those squirrelly dogs that always seem to be named Muffy."

"Yeah, squeaky little fur balls!"

"Hey!" Dominic grabbed a pencil from his pocket and asked, "Do you ever do riddles?" He took Cricket's napkin and drew nine circles, three across the top, three in the middle, and three on the bottom. Next he drew a square around all nine circles.

"Say these are balls," he began, scooting so close that his knee practically touched hers. "Now, you want to keep the balls from rolling together, but instead of making a box for each ball, they can be kept apart by drawing just two squares. Can you do it?"

"I don't know." She took the pencil and tapped it against her teeth. "Can they be rectangles?"

"Nope. Want me to show you?"

Cricket shot up her hand. "Wait a second—give

me a chance. Let's see, two squares . . . no, that's not right."

While she erased a line, Dominic leaned on an elbow and watched her, grinning.

Cricket looked up and pointed the tip of the pencil at him. "If you think you're so smart, try doing this one. Okay, there was this man and his son, and they're driving along, when suddenly their car hits a tree. The boy's father is pinned inside the car. An ambulance comes and takes his kid away—"

"This is a happy story."

"Stop it," Cricket said, lightly punching his arm. "Everything turns out fine. Anyway, they take the kid to the hospital and wheel him straight into an operating room. The surgeon is there, all done up in a green mask and rubber gloves, when suddenly the surgeon leans over, takes a close look at the kid, and says, 'I can't operate on that boy, he's my son.' How can that be?"

Squinting his eyes, Dominic focused on a corner of the ceiling. "Well, is the surgeon the boy's stepfather? Or was the kid adopted?"

"Nope."

"Let's see then, did the dad in the car jump in a helicopter real fast and fly to the hospital?"

Cricket giggled, "No, no, no. Think a minute. It's obvious if you use your brain."

He grabbed the napkin, waved it under her nose, and said, "I don't see you figuring out your puzzle, either."

"Okay," Cricket replied, shoving away the tray, "you do yours and I'll do mine." They were both so intent on their puzzles that they didn't hear Joey Jenkowitz come up from behind.

"Dominic, we're waiting for you outside." Joey was Crackerbox, and looked it. Shoving his hands in his pockets, he rolled onto the heels of his sneakers and said, "Recess'll be over in a minute."

"I gotta go," Dominic told her. "But first, let me give you the answer real quick." He took the pencil and drew a tilted square around five of the balls, then made a smaller square in the center.

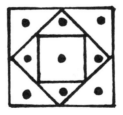

"I didn't get it at first, either," he told her as he grabbed his lunchbox. "Someone had to show me, too."

"Come *on,* Dominic!" Joey demanded.

"Okay. See you outside, Cricket!"

"Wait," Cricket cried, "you didn't guess the answer to your riddle. . . ." But he was already gone.

She watched as Dominic and Joey hurried out to the playground. Dominic had been there only a little over a week, and already he had more friends than she did. Even though he'd seemed like a nothing that first day, he'd somehow managed to turn things around. It's because he's Crackerbox, she told herself. Crackerbox kids always stick together. But even as she thought it, Cricket knew it wasn't true. Dominic made friends because he was just plain nice.

Later that evening, Cricket curled at the foot of her father's desk and browsed through a book of riddles she'd checked from the school library. It was quiet in his study; the green glass lamp cast shadows across airplane, business, and hunting books that lined the heavy walnut shelves.

"Here's one," Cricket told Treasure, rubbing the dog's fur with one hand while balancing the book on her knees. "What has a foot on each end and one in the middle? A yardstick. What do you think, Treasure, too easy?"

Treasure squeezed a chew toy shaped like a hot dog between her paws and gnawed on the end.

"Okay, try this. What doesn't think or speak, but always tells the truth? A good scale. My mom'd love that one."

The phone rang, making her jump.

"Cricket!" Her mother's voice floated down the hall. "It's for you."

"For me?" Reaching over her head, Cricket grabbed for the phone. It was shaped like a mallard duck.

"Hello?"

"Cricket? It's me. Dominic."

For a reason she couldn't explain, Cricket felt her stomach squeeze. "Oh. Hi."

"Listen," he said, "you never told me the answer to your riddle. I thought of something, but I'm not sure. Was the surgeon a priest? You know, like if it were a priest he'd be everybody's father, and then he might call the boy 'my son'. . . ."

"No." Cricket laughed. "It's the kid's *mother*. A surgeon can be a woman, you know."

"Oh, yeah! I didn't think of that."

There was a pause. Cricket wasn't used to talking on the phone. It seemed like Dominic wasn't comfortable, either.

"Well," he said, "I think I'll go and try out your riddle on my mom. It's really a good one. See you tomorrow, Cricket."

"Okay," Cricket said. "Bye."

After she'd hung up, she lifted Treasure's ears high, then let them flop back down. "You know, Treas, if you ever met Dominic, I bet you'd like him."

Treasure flicked her head toward Cricket. Her eyes seemed to widen.

"But don't worry, there's never going to be anyone I want to be with as much as you." After scratching the soft patch under Treasure's collar, Cricket rolled onto her stomach, crossed her ankles, and searched the book for another good riddle.

8

Flakes of snow spun lightly to the ground, melting as soon as they touched the asphalt. Cricket leaned against the school wall, hands clasped to the small of her back, and watched Dominic hit a tetherball. It was the middle of November, and pretty soon the tetherballs would be taken down until spring. All the kids seemed to want to play one last time. Dominic's breath made little puffs of steam every time he smacked the ball. She'd never tried it before, but now it almost looked fun.

"Hey, Cricket," Dominic called out. "You any good at this?"

Cricket's eyes widened. What were they like down in Florida? Did he think because he'd called her last night, he could act friendly in public and let the whole world know? No boy at Woodland ever asked a girl to play tetherball, especially in front of other kids.

"She's not any good," Ryan yelled. "She's afraid she'll muss up her hair."

Ryan shook his head wildly, then ran his fingers through white blond locks. In a falsetto voice he cried, "Oh, my, I think I broke a nail!"

"Sure, I'll play." Cricket could hardly believe she'd said it.

"Great. Do you know how?"

"You hit the ball till the string wraps to the top of the pole. The one whose side it ends up on wins. I'm not stupid."

"She just tries to look that way," Ryan offered.

Dominic gave him a look. "Okay, Cricket. You start."

She hit the ball with the palm of her hand. It barely arched to Dominic's side.

Ryan sneered, "Such power. Awesome!"

Dominic threw the ball back and said, "Don't be scared of it. Really hit the sucker."

Cricket balled her hand into a fist. This time she

gave it a good hard smack. It whirled around to Dominic's side.

"Great." He hit the ball gently back to her.

"Looks like I'm watching fairy-ball!"

"Knock it off, Ryan. Okay, Cricket, I'm ready."

"Ready for what? More tether-puff? You know, Dominic, you sure picked a loser for a girlfriend. Everyone in school thinks Cricket's got the biggest mouth—"

Ryan didn't finish his sentence. Instead of hitting the ball, Dominic turned around and gave Ryan a shove. "I said, knock it off!"

Ryan grabbed Dominic's arm and spun him to the ground. In a flash Ryan jumped on top of him.

"Fight! Fight!" Candie screamed. Instantly a crowd gathered at the center of the playground. Dominic and Ryan rolled across the gravel, their legs beating the air, fists flying. Cricket watched in horror. Boys were so stupid! How could they actually hit each other? They rocked back and forth until Ryan managed to flip on top. A thin ribbon of blood trickled from his nose. His fist clenched, ready to land a punch on Dominic's face. Without realizing what she was doing, Cricket lunged forward and jumped on Ryan's back.

"Stop hitting him!" she screamed. She pulled

his hair, Ryan reared back, and Cricket fell hard onto her bottom.

"What is the meaning of this!"

Like magic the crowd moved apart. From the ground, their principal, Mr. Hadshaw, looked ten feet tall.

"You three, get up! I want you all in my office. *Now!*"

"Ryan Jones?" Mr. Hadshaw's secretary announced, "You may go in now."

The three of them sat in a row in Mr. Hadshaw's stuffy outer office. Ryan, arms crossed, eyes straight ahead, slumped into his chair. His legs stuck straight out in front, like two Chinese chopsticks; his nose was pink and slightly swollen; a knuckle on his left hand looked raw.

"Which one of you is Ryan?" the secretary asked.

Cricket and Dominic pointed. Ryan scowled.

"This way now. Mr. Hadshaw is waiting."

As he heaved himself to his feet, Ryan leaned over Dominic and Cricket.

"You swung first. I hope Hadshaw fries your butt."

"I hope you're suspended the rest of your life!"

Cricket hissed back. Dominic said nothing.

As Ryan disappeared into Hadshaw's office, the secretary followed and shut the door quietly behind them. Cricket heard the murmur of voices inside.

"I've never really been in trouble before," Cricket said softly. "What's going to happen now?"

"How would I know?" Dominic snapped.

"Because . . ." She faltered. "I guess I thought from the way you flattened Ryan . . ."

"Well, I've never hit anyone before in my life." He narrowed his eyes and added, "Not counting my sister."

A scrape stretched from Dominic's right eye to the corner of his mouth; his knee poked through a tear in his faded jeans. He tugged at the hole, then licked the palm of his hand and ran it over the top of his head. "Do you think I look okay? I don't want Mr. Hadshaw to think I'm a JD."

"What's a JD?"

"A juvenile delinquent."

Cricket's gaze started at his feet, then swept to his face and back down to his shoes. Dominic seemed uncomfortable at her staring. His jaw tensed as he waited for her to answer. He was pretty ragged, Cricket thought, but there was nothing much he could do about it so she said, "You look fine."

Shifting in the hard wooden seat, Cricket winced as she tried to find a comfortable spot. Her behind was sore from the way she'd landed. She had no idea cold asphalt could be so hard.

"What's the matter, Cricket? Did you get hurt?"

Cricket thought of her sore bottom. No matter how nice Dominic was, there were some things she just couldn't tell a boy.

"Nope. Not a bit," she lied.

Dominic pulled at the tips of his fingers. He cleared his throat. He tapped the sides of his shoes together as though they were castanets.

"If I'm late from school again, Treasure will get into some kind of trouble," Cricket said, trying to distract him from the voices growing louder behind Hadshaw's door. "You know what she did yesterday? She grabbed the end of the toilet paper and unwound it. Really, she did! It looked like a mummy died in my bathroom."

"That's really funny, Cricket." He looked so nervous that she tried again.

"Oh, I've got another riddle. If you have a hole that's one foot square, and one foot deep, then exactly how much dirt is in it?"

"None," he said, his voice flat. "If it's a hole, it's empty."

"I guess you already heard it."

"Yeah." Dominic sighed deeply, then turned to look at her. "The thing is, I just don't want to be in trouble my first week at Woodland. My dad'll kill me."

Was he blaming her for the fight? Cricket wondered. Was he sorry now that he'd taken her side?

"At my old school, I was on the honor roll. I hope this won't keep me off Woodland's."

So, now it was her fault if he didn't make the honor roll!

"Well," Cricket flared, "if you're so worried about being in trouble, why did you shove Ryan in the first place?"

"I don't know." He crossed his arms over his chest. Next he crossed his legs.

Cricket got a sinking feeling in her stomach. He was blaming her, she knew it! She could tell just by looking at his face!

"It's not my fault, Dominic. I didn't ask to play tetherball. I didn't ask you to shove Ryan!"

"I know that!"

"Then why'd you do it?"

"I did it because . . ." Dominic's face flushed.

"I guess because I don't like it when someone's a jerk to one of my friends."

Friends! A picture of Melanie and Heather and Skye flashed through Cricket's mind. She thought of all the other Crackerbox kids, of all the kids from Pepperwood, and even of Whitney, and then she pictured Dominic. He seemed to like her even when she hadn't done anything special. She didn't know why he liked her, but she knew he did. He was right—they really were friends!

Just then, the door to Mr. Hadshaw's room swung open and Ryan shuffled out. He didn't look too happy.

"Kristin Winslow," the secretary called.

She was next. She'd have to explain everything to stone-faced Mr. Hadshaw. He might call her mother and would certainly send home a note. Cricket drew in a deep breath and stood. She should have been scared, really scared, but she knew that when she walked back out, Dominic would be there. And somehow, that made all the difference.

9

"It's right down this street," Dominic said, ducking his head against the cold. "The one with the blue truck out front."

Cricket hesitated. She could really get into trouble for going to Dominic's house, especially because she hadn't asked her mother first. Lois hadn't liked the idea at all. As the window of the Mercedes slid open Lois had leaned out, giving Dominic the once-over. Her mouth looked grim.

"Don't worry," Cricket had assured her. "I'll call Mom as soon as I get there. I'm sure it will be fine!"

Lois narrowed her eyes. She seemed to focus

on the hole in Dominic's glove. And the ink stain on the pocket of his jacket. In a tone as cold as the November air, she'd said, "Is he the one who started that fight on Friday?"

"I explained that already." Slipping a paper with the address into Lois's hand, she said, "I'm doing a report for class, and if I get a bad grade, Mom'll *really* be mad. This is homework!" As Dominic fidgeted, Cricket wailed, "Come on, Lois, give me a break!"

Lois studied Dominic one more time. Cricket could tell she was hesitating.

"Okay. But your folks better not mind! If they do, it's on your head!"

She'd pressed a button, and the window glided halfway up. "I don't want you working any later than five-thirty. Got that? Five-thirty! Now get in and I'll drive you to Dominic's."

Dominic hung back, almost as though he were afraid of the silver Mercedes. He kept punching the toe of his boot into a crust of snow.

"That's okay," Cricket had said quickly. "We sort of wanted to walk."

"What?"

"Walk. Everybody else does. I've got legs; I can do it."

Lois's mouth parted, like a fish. Finally she'd

said, "Go right ahead. My kids walked every day, and it didn't hurt them. I just hope you know what you're doing."

Cricket had flashed a brilliant smile. "Thanks, Lois. I'll call Mom the minute I get there. Give Treasure a hug for me and tell her I'll be back soon, okay? Bye!"

And now she was walking down a narrow road, in a place totally different from Pepperwood. Whenever they'd driven by, Cricket had thought the Crackerbox houses looked small and tidy, like the little Christmas village they placed under their tree. But up close they seemed tired and lumpy. The paint on the porches was chipped. Weathered wooden fences butted against rusted chain link. Winter-bare trees touched branches, as though they were holding bony hands. Even the snow looked gray.

"What are you looking at?" Dominic's voice cut into her thoughts.

"I don't know. Nothing."

"It's different than Yuppiewood, right?"

Cricket looked at him.

"Yuppiewood? What's Yuppiewood?"

"You know what a yuppie is, don't you?" Dominic asked. His brown eyes widened, like he was surprised, but his mouth was a straight line.

Cricket stared at him blankly. "No. But it sounds like a disease."

Dominic rubbed the tips of his ears with his hands to keep them warm. His nose was running. "You could call it a disease. A money disease. My dad told me all about it. Yuppie stands for Young, Upper something something. . . . I can't remember exactly. . . ."

Cricket stopped walking. She put her hands on her hips. She wasn't quite sure what he was saying, but she knew she didn't like it.

"I don't know what Upper something something means," she said, trying to sound as cool as her mother did in court. "Do you?"

"No."

"Then why did you bring it up?"

Dominic dug his hands into his pockets. Then he looked straight at her.

"My house is just as good as yours. It might not be as big, but it keeps the snow off our heads just the same."

Wrinkling her nose, Cricket said, "You sound like somebody else. Did your dad tell you to say that?"

"No." Dominic flushed. "He just says that all the time."

"Well, it sounds stupid," Cricket declared. "I

don't know what you're worried about, but I'm cold."

"Okay. But don't expect a maid in a Mercedes."

The air inside the Falcone home was warm and steamy. Mrs. Falcone stood in the kitchen, clucking over a bubbling pot as a baby at her feet threw noodles onto the floor.

The first thing that Cricket noticed about the Falcone home was the smell. Her house in Pepperwood smelled clean, like pine and furniture polish. But to Cricket, this place smelled like heaven. The aroma of garlic, tomatoes, and sausage, mingled with onion and olive oil, wafted across the room. Two scented spice candles stood on either side of a cornucopia; a pot of coffee percolated on top of their stove. She breathed deeply. How would it be to live in a house brimming with such delicious odors?

Mrs. Falcone caught sight of the two of them. She broke into a big smile.

"Hey, Dominic, you're home!" she cried. "And this must be Cricket! Come in! Take off your boots; get out of the cold!"

She motioned them inside with a hand that held a baby bottle.

"Shut the door, Nicky. I can't afford to heat the whole outdoors!"

Cricket studied Mrs. Falcone as she unzipped her boots. She was so different from her own mother. Cricket's mother was pencil thin, while Dominic's mother was soft and round, like a bunch of pillows stacked one on top of the other. Her pants were black polyester; a top with blue roses hung loosely to her hips. Her hair was short and curly, dark like her son's, and when she smiled, her cheeks crinkled.

Dominic's boots landed in the entryway with a thud. Cricket set hers neatly to the side.

"Hey, Mom, got anything to eat?" Dominic yelled.

"Would you come home if I didn't? Sit down at the table. I made some sandwiches."

Cricket followed Dominic into their tiny kitchen, wondering if she could ask to hold the baby, but Mrs. Falcone waved them toward a large, oval table. Two vinyl place mats had already been set out.

"Here you go. Now don't forget your manners, Dominic. Cricket should choose first."

Never before in her whole life had Cricket seen sandwiches like these. White bread, cheese, mayonnaise, thick slices of turkey and roast beef that didn't come from packages, surrounded by a ring of fresh grapes, apples, and orange slices. She picked a turkey sandwich, then waited for Dominic. He picked beef.

"Here, have some milk. There's cookies when you're done. I'll be out in the living room, folding clothes. Come on, Teresa," Mrs. Falcone said, sweeping the baby into her arms. "Let's leave these two to work."

"Can I see the baby, just for a second?" Cricket begged. "She's darling!"

"Sure. This is Teresa. She's eleven months old. She'd like to stay and play with you, but she's due for a nap right now. Say bye-bye to Cricket, Teresa."

The little baby waved a chubby fist at Cricket and ducked her head into her mother's shoulder. The two of them disappeared down the hall.

Cricket studied the plate of food. "Do you always eat like this?" she whispered.

"Only when we have company. I told her you were coming today." Dominic took a big bite of his sandwich.

"I didn't even know I was coming."

"I took a chance."

Cricket bit into her sandwich. It was delicious.

She chewed slowly, savoring every mouthful.

"Did you start on the written report?" Dominic asked.

"Um-hmmm. It's really interesting. I never knew what made a dog a purebred before. It reminded me to ask you if you had one. A dog, I mean." As she talked Cricket glanced around the room, her gaze resting on plastic butterflies, plastic fruit, and pictures with gold plastic frames.

"Whenever I eat," she went on, eyeing crayon squiggles the baby must have drawn on the wall, "Treasure sticks her nose in my lap and stares up at me until I give her some food. She begs so much she's getting fat as a—"

When Cricket saw Dominic, she stopped talking.

An expression of sadness, mixed with anger, clouded his face.

"What's wrong?"

"Nothing. It's just . . . I did have a dog. I got her when I was in Florida. Then our neighbors lost her, and I never saw her again."

"Oh."

"I'd like to get another dog, but my dad says I'll have to wait. He says he doesn't want to housebreak a puppy in the winter."

"What does your dad do?" Cricket asked,

changing the subject. She didn't like to see Dominic look so unhappy. Especially since she had Treasure.

"My dad? He's a policeman."

"Really? Does he drive around in a squad car? Has he ever been shot?"

Dominic grinned, then took another sip of milk. "Stuff like that only happens on TV. He's a detective now, anyway. That's the reason we moved out here, on account of his promotion. Where does your dad work?"

"Up in the sky."

"Huh?"

"You *said* where. He's a pilot, so he works *in* the sky. It's a joke, Dominic."

Rolling his eyes, Dominic exclaimed, "A joke! Now I get it. I'm glad you told me, 'cause I always thought a joke had to be funny. A joke—ha ha ha!"

Cricket made a face. "Shut up, *Nicky.*"

"Yes, your bugginess."

They both laughed. Dominic got up and cleared their plates, then threw a stack of books and papers onto the table. Cricket watched him, and inside her, warm feelings bubbled up like the Falcone soup pot. It was fun being here, being fed, having someone to talk to.

78

"Oh, I've got another riddle for you," Cricket said. "What goes up the chimney down, and down the chimney down, but can't go up the chimney up or down the chimney up?"

"Huh?"

"An umbrella!" She grinned. "Get it?"

"We'd better get *down* to work," Dominic said, rolling his eyes, "before our time's all *up*. Let's start with deciding who's going to draw what."

Half an hour later, Dominic tossed his pencil in the air and caught it with his left hand. "Want to stop now? How are you at Monopoly?"

Cricket crossed her arms. "Deadly."

"We'll see."

He went to a cupboard and rummaged until he found an old, taped Monopoly box. In Cricket's game, the money was crisp and smooth, so that it lay in perfect money stacks. The bills he counted out were smudged and wrinkled. They must play this game a lot, Cricket thought.

They were deep into the game when his four-year-old sister burst through the back door and demanded to play.

"But Camille, this is Monopoly. You're not big enough," Dominic protested. "And besides, Cricket doesn't want to play with a little squirt like you."

Camille turned two large brown eyes on Cricket. Black ringlets tumbled to her shoulders, freckles sprinkled the bridge of her nose, and her cheeks were fat. Cricket thought she was adorable.

"What do you want to do, Camille?" she asked, squatting down to her level.

"I want to hide and seek, in the basement. That way it's more scarier."

"It's okay with me. Why don't you and I go hide, and then Dominic will have to find us!"

Shrugging his shoulders, Dominic sighed, "One time. I'll only look for you one time, and then we'll come back and finish our game. You're doing this 'cause I'm creaming you at Monopoly, right?"

"No I'm not! I've never had a brother or a sister to play with. It sounds like fun."

"You're crazy," Dominic snorted.

"Can we hide now?" Camille begged.

She took Camille's hand and descended the rickety stairs that lead to their basement. It *was* a scary place to hide. The small bulb that hung from the rafters barely lit the room. Deep shadows filled every corner. A stuffed deer head, piles of boxes, four old steamer trunks, bicycles, and dusty furniture were stacked everywhere. There were hundreds of good hiding places to choose from.

"Now be real quiet, okay, Camille?" Cricket whispered. "Let's see if we can play a trick on Nicky."

Camille nodded solemnly. She'd followed Cricket's every move without a sound.

"This looks good," Cricket told her. "You go first."

The two of them crawled into a large, half-empty box turned on one side.

Dominic's footsteps thundered down the stairs. "Ready or not you shall be caught!"

Cricket heard the squeak of his sneakers on the cement floor as he walked closer to their hiding place. "Shhh," she breathed to Camille.

Just as Dominic passed the box, Cricket reached out her hand and grabbed his ankle.

"Aaaaaah!" Dominic screamed. He jumped like a rocket, Camille squealed, and Cricket laughed until tears rolled from her eyes.

"Oh, you think you're so funny, but now it's your turn!" he warned. Cricket ran upstairs and began to count. Monopoly lay on the table, forgotten.

After seven games, they took a break. Dominic poured them drinks in pastel Tupperware tumblers. A horn blared in the driveway, and Mrs. Falcone called, "Nicky, Cricket's mother is here!"

Sheepishly, Dominic looked at the stack of papers shoved to the back of the counter and said, "We didn't work too hard on our project. You want to come back tomorrow?"

"Sure! That sounds great! But would you like to come to my house?"

He looked at the floor. He took a breath to say something, then clapped his mouth shut.

"Come see me again," Camille begged. "You're fun!"

"Maybe," Dominic began, finally looking up, "we should do it here. 'Cause of Camille. If that's okay with you."

So, Cricket realized, he felt funny about coming to her house. Probably because she was Pepperwood. She guessed it didn't matter, as long as she still had time for Treasure.

"Here is fine."

"Okay!" he smiled. "Tomorrow we'll really go to it. Thanks for coming over, Cricket. It was . . . fun."

"For me, too." Cricket felt suddenly shy. But, she told herself, she was here on business. They had a report to do! And secretly, she hoped it would take them a long, long time.

"Would you stop sniffing me?" Cricket complained as she and Treasure curled into bed. "You're driving me crazy. It's like sleeping with a vacuum cleaner."

Treasure's wet nose puffed over her hand, up her arm, and tickled through her hair. It made Cricket laugh, but she was tired and wanted to get some sleep.

Whining, Treasure pawed the comforter.

"Look, I'm asleep already. Good night, Treasure." Cricket squeezed her eyes shut. She didn't hear a sound. Through fluttering lids, she took a tiny, careful peek. Treasure sat, head cocked, watching her.

"Oh, Treasure," she groaned, "would you just lie down? Please?"

Pulling Treasure's head onto her pillow, Cricket wrapped her arms around her dog and went to sleep. That night, she dreamed of Dominic, of a baby and a little girl with black ringlets, and of thick sandwiches made with cheese.

10

"Excellent job, Cricket! Dominic, I can see how much work went into this project. Well done!" Mrs. Chumley announced. "You even made a chart. Lovely!"

It was 7:52 A.M. Class wouldn't start for another eight minutes, but Dominic and Cricket had decided to meet early to set up their project. Mrs. Chumley took a metal stand out of her closet and placed it at the front of the classroom.

"You can put your poster right up here. Oooh, I like the spikes on the dog collar."

"Dominic did that," Cricket offered. "I drew the poodle."

"Well, I'm sure the class will enjoy your report. Now aren't you glad I put the two of you together? You see, sometimes teachers are smart after all!"

Mrs. Chumley was right; it *was* good to work with Dominic. Cricket had never tried so hard on anything in her life as she had on that dog report. And it showed. The feeling of pride would have been perfect except for a little fear tugging at the corner of her heart: Now that their project was done, she'd no longer have any excuse to be with Dominic.

The last three weeks had been the happiest time of her life. Almost every day Mrs. Falcone had made a plate of food, and they'd eaten, then worked for a while, then played. Once they'd made a haunted house. Another time Dominic unearthed an old bowling ball, so they set up an alley with empty Clorox bottles for pins.

The Falcone house was noisy, cluttered, a little dusty, and a whole lot of fun. Cricket loved it. For the first time she could remember, she felt as though she had it all. She'd wanted a dog more than anything, and she'd gotten it. She'd wanted a friend, and Dominic appeared. Everything in her life was perfect, would continue to be perfect, if only it stayed just the way it was. But what if Dominic didn't invite her over again? She watched him tuck his shirttail into the back of his new pair of tan cords. It was true that he'd said they were friends, but what would happen now that their excuse to be together was gone?

"Dominic, I was just thinking," Cricket said slowly. "You know a lot about dogs, and you haven't even met mine. My dog, I mean."

He stopped adjusting the chart and turned to look at her.

"So, anyway, I thought if you weren't busy, after school, that maybe you could come over to my house and meet Treasure."

There. She'd said it. Cricket could hear the voices of the other kids echoing in the hallway. She wished Dominic would hurry up and say something, instead of just standing there with his mouth hanging open.

"You can hear, can't you? Hello! Dominic!" she waved her arms at him.

"Sure," he finally said. "I can come over. If your folks won't mind."

Cricket felt a rush of relief. He still wanted to be with her after all.

"Great! After school, then."

At that moment Heather walked into the room. Her long hair was pulled up in a side ponytail. Red, white, and green satin ribbons were tied an inch apart all the way down her hair. It was eighteen days until Christmas; from years past Cricket knew Heather would wear only holiday colors all December long.

"Hi Cricket, hi Duminic," Heather said, dumping her binder on her desk. She always said his name like that, and every time she did, Dominic stiffened. Cricket was really beginning to hate her. Heather walked over to their poster, stopped, twisted her hair around her finger and asked, "Is this *the* project? Who did the punk collar on the dog? That is a dog, isn't it?"

"No, it's a picture of you," Cricket answered sweetly. "Your name is on every other spike!"

"Oh, real funny," Heather snapped.

"You don't have to thank us," Cricket declared. "We're always glad to do a little something for a big nothing."

Heather spun around so hard her ponytail stood out like a candy cane. She stomped off to her desk. Lately Melanie, Heather, and Skye had been especially rude to Cricket, and now that she had her own real friend, Cricket was more than happy to hand it back.

"I don't think I'd ever want to get on your bad side," Dominic said under his breath. "You can be nasty!"

Cricket giggled. "I'm not mean!"

"I still wouldn't want to fight you."

Punching his arm, Cricket said, "There's nothing for us to fight about!"

Dominic grinned. Cricket grinned back.

She couldn't know just how wrong she was.

11

THEIR HOUSE LOOKED LIKE CHRISTMAS. ON EACH side of the double door, Cricket's mother had hung enormous wreaths, heavy with apples and red velvet ribbons. The rooftop, the windows, even the fir trees were strung with white lights, and at night it seemed as though the stars were sprinkled across their home. This year, her mother had chosen to decorate the Christmas tree in pure white. White feather doves, white lights, and strand after strand of white pearls encircled the tree, right up to the silvery angel. Cricket could hardly wait for Dominic to see it.

Lois pushed a button that automatically opened their garage door.

"Treasure will be right inside," Cricket bubbled to Dominic.

"No, she won't," Lois said, without turning around. "I just washed the kitchen floor, so I put her in the basement. You know how she leaves paw prints in the fresh wax!"

"Well, it'll only take me a second to get her then. Usually she's standing guard, ready to bounce me when I come in."

Dominic nodded his head. "My dog used to do that, too. Her name was Coty. She used to jump all over me the minute I opened the door."

Cricket couldn't help but notice how sad Dominic looked when he thought of his lost dog. But that didn't matter. Soon the two of them could play with Treasure as long as they wanted.

"This is just the garage," Cricket went on as she got out of the car.

"Is that your bike?" Dominic asked in a hushed voice.

"Both of them are. They're just bikes."

Suddenly Cricket felt a little uncomfortable. Her house was a lot bigger than Dominic's, and she had a lot more things. She didn't want him to think she was showing off. "Hey, here's another riddle," she said as Dominic's gaze wandered across the power boat parked in the corner of their garage.

"There was a guy named Joe Smith. Every night, he got into an elevator and rode up to the eighth floor," Cricket said. "Then he'd get off and walk the stairs clear up to the fifteenth floor, which was where he lived."

Dominic looked behind him, at the lawn mower her father rode when he cut their grass.

"Anyway, you're supposed to figure out why Joe didn't just ride straight to the fifteenth floor."

"I don't know," Dominic said quietly.

"It's because Joe Smith was only six years old! See, he couldn't reach any higher than the eighth button. . . . Oh, never mind."

"That's a good one. Let's go in."

"And this is the kitchen. It doesn't smell good, like yours," Cricket told him. "Let me just show you the Christmas tree while Lois lets Treasure out. My mom picked a white theme for our tree this year."

As she talked, Dominic followed her from room to room. His eyes widened at the vaulted ceilings, the thick wooden molding, and elegant oriental rugs.

"You've got the kind of carpet that leaves footprints when you walk," Dominic stated.

"Yeah, well, Lois follows everyone around with a vacuum cleaner. One time she made me walk backwards out of the living room so I wouldn't leave extra footprints!" She meant it to be funny, but Dominic wasn't laughing. He really seemed uneasy.

"I can see why you need a maid. This place is really big."

"It's not that big," Cricket protested. But she knew that to Dominic, it probably was.

"You'd need a map just to find the bathroom," he murmured.

"No, you don't. Second door on the left."

"I bet you've got one of those bathtubs with a whirlpool in it, right? No, in this place I bet you've got a whole swimming pool in there!"

She pretended to kick him. "Hey, I didn't make fun of your house."

"I'm not making fun, it's just . . . *big*!"

"Well, stop saying that. The truth is, this place isn't half as nice as your house!"

Dominic snorted. "Yeah, right. Wanna trade?"

"No, I mean I would in a second. You should see my refrigerator. All we've got is yogurt and healthy stuff. This isn't so great. If it weren't for Treasure . . . well, it's empty."

"I think I could stand it."

Cricket didn't know if she should go on. They were in the living room, and their twelve-foot tree stood shimmering in the corner. She bent down and plugged in the lights. If he wanted to be a pain about her house, she guessed it was all right. He'd get used to it in a minute. She just wished he'd stop making such a big deal about it.

"Well, this is the tree. Last year it was blue—not the tree, the ornaments, I mean. And the year before it was red and the year before that . . ."

Cricket didn't get to finish. She heard Treasure yapping in the hallway. Good. Now maybe Dominic could say something besides the word *big*. She turned just in time to see Treasure freeze at the entryway.

Dominic stood for a moment like a statue. Cricket's eyes darted from Treasure to Dominic and back to Treasure again.

"Here, Treasure. Come here, girl," Cricket called. But Treasure stood still, her whiskers barely trembling on her soft muzzle. Something was wrong. Something was terribly, terribly wrong.

"Come here, girl," Cricket cried.

"Coty!"

Dominic's voice was choked, but it broke the

spell. Treasure leaped against him, her body dancing as she caressed his face with kisses.

"Oh, Coty, you're back. Oh, Coty girl, I missed you so much. Cricket, this is Coty! I can't even believe it! You found my dog!"

12

"WHERE DID YOU FIND HER?" DOMINIC ASKED, HIS eyes glowing.

"I found Treasure at the pound. But she's not your dog, Dominic, she's mine."

Treasure broke away from Dominic, barking and jumping in joyful circles. He grabbed her and rubbed her back furiously. "Oh, girl, it's so good to see you. I thought you were gone forever!"

"Your dog must have *looked* like mine, but . . ."

Shaking his head, Dominic declared, "No, this is Coty all right. You think she'd jump all over me if it weren't Coty? Wait'll my dad sees her! He's going to flip out!"

Panic welled inside Cricket. She couldn't lose Treasure! She wouldn't! Pictures buzzed through her mind: Treasure growling and snapping at her sock, or curled into a warm ball at the foot of her bed. Treasure out on walks, her nose burrowing in fresh drifts of snow. Treasure, paws perched on the windowsill, waiting for Cricket to walk inside. That was her dog, hers and no one else's. But that same dog, her Treasure, hadn't stopped nuzzling Dominic's face. And that made her cold with fear.

Suddenly an idea flashed through her mind. She snapped her fingers and cried, "Wait a minute! You said you lost your dog in Florida, all the way across the country. I found her before you even moved here. Treasure couldn't be yours!" Relief washed over her. It was simple! Florida was two thousand miles away. He'd lost his dog in Florida; therefore, Treasure couldn't be his. She let out a breath she hadn't known she was holding. Maybe, Cricket thought, she'd be a lawyer when she grew up. The key was to think logically.

She expected Dominic to look deflated, but he was smiling so hard it seemed his cheeks would pop right off his face.

"No, that's not what I said. I said I lost my dog

when I *went* to Florida. See, me and my dad and Coty drove out here to look for a house. My Mom had to stay back in Florida 'cause Camille was real sick. So anyway, we found a house and then left Coty out here with a friend of my dad's."

Now it was Cricket who deflated. She bit her lip, then asked, "Why didn't you take your dog back to Florida with you? That seems pretty mean to just dump her with strangers."

"I didn't want to leave her, but my dad said we didn't have room to make the trip with the whole family and Coty too. And anyway, it was only supposed to be for a few days. But she ran away. By the time we got back, it was too late."

His face broke into another brilliant smile. "I am so glad you found her! This is so great!" One hand scratched under Treasure's chin while the other glided down her sides. "Looks like you've had the royal treatment, huh, girl? You've gained a pound or two since you've been here. I bet you got more than just plain old dry dog food. . . ."

Cricket stomped her foot so hard ornaments quivered on the frosted tree. "Treasure's not fat and she's not leaving my house!" Her voice was louder than she'd wanted, but Dominic had kept babbling about Treasure as though she were already his. Suddenly, the room seemed deathly quiet. Dominic looked over Treasure's head and stared.

"Are you crazy?" he breathed. "You can tell she's my dog."

Cricket narrowed her eyes. "Stop saying that. She's not your dog; she's mine!"

His hand stopped rubbing Treasure's coat. His jaw squared.

"Get real, Cricket. Just look at her. Does this look like a dog that doesn't know me?"

"She's just friendly, that's all," Cricket shot back. "Treasure does that to everyone."

"Her name is Coty!"

"It's Treasure!"

Treasure began to whine. Her small stub of a tail was tucked between shivering legs, but she stayed rooted at Dominic's side.

"She'd come to me if you'd stop grabbing her. Let her *go*! Here, Treasure! Treasure, *come here*!" She slapped her thighs so hard they burned. "Leave Dominic *alone*!"

Quaking like a tree in a whirlwind, Treasure whined, but didn't move. Cricket stomped across the room, slipped her fingers under her collar, and yanked her away from Dominic.

Dominic's eyes flashed. "Hey, knock it off, Cricket. I haven't seen Coty in a long time!"

"Treasure! Her name is Treasure! Are you deaf or something?"

Treasure jumped on Cricket. She nuzzled her face, then arched her body toward Dominic.

"See, she wants me," he declared.

Cricket's voice was ice. "I don't care. I bought her. That makes her mine. Got that? *Mine!*"

Dominic walked over to where Cricket was standing. He seemed bigger than he ever had, but Cricket wasn't afraid. She was too scared of losing Treasure.

"I bought her first. She's a registered springer spaniel, and she's registered to *me*. And I'm taking her home!"

Treasure wiggled frantically from Cricket to Dominic. They were standing close enough to touch, with Treasure wedged between them.

"Get out of here!" Cricket screamed, pulling on Treasure's collar.

Dominic yanked her back and yelled, "I'm not going without my dog!"

"What is going on in here?" Lois demanded. "I could hear you all the way in the basement! What are you two fighting about?"

"Dominic's trying to take my dog away," Cricket cried, clutching Treasure. Her throat felt so tight she thought she might not be able to

99

speak. Dominic looked both angry and embarrassed.

"Is that true?" Lois asked sternly.

"No, this is my dog. I want her back."

Slowly Lois crossed her arms. Her voice dropped low as she said, "I think you'd better leave now. Get your coat."

Dominic looked from Treasure to Cricket to Lois. He let go of Treasure, then backed away. "I'll leave Coty for now. I'm going to get Coty's papers, and then I'll be back, with my dad."

He ran to their front door, then turned to Cricket with a look of defiance. "You know, Cricket, I thought we were friends. But you're just as stuck on yourself as all the other rich brats." He pulled his coat under his chin, all the while staring angrily at Cricket.

"I'll take you home," Lois offered.

"No, thanks. I'll be back, Cricket." The door slammed behind him. Christmas bells that dangled from the doorknob rang harshly, slapping against the wood.

"Well, at least he's gone," Lois sighed. Suddenly Treasure bolted from Cricket's arms, barking and whining at the window.

"Oh, Lois, what am I going to do?" Cricket

cried. Her voice broke as she tried to swallow the sob pushing up through her chest.

"Just wait for your parents, honey. They'll know what's right."

"What if they don't? What if they say to give her back?"

Treasure's whining became low, pain-filled moans. "Don't cry," Cricket said, running to her dog. She clutched Treasure tightly around the middle and whispered, "Please don't cry. I'm still here." One by one Cricket's tears disappeared into the dog's soft fur.

"Oh, Treasure, I just can't lose you. Not ever. I love you."

Treasure stood as still as the wooden animals around the Christmas manger.

13

CRICKET STOOD AT THE WINDOW, WAITING FOR HER mother's BMW to swing up the drive. It was almost seven o'clock. In the halo of their outdoor lights she could see tiny flakes of snow drift gently to the ground. Her dad was out of town, again, and her mother was late. Tapping fingernails against the sill, Cricket wished for the hundredth time that her mother would hurry. Dominic had said he'd be back; Cricket knew he meant it.

Strains of "Silent Night" played softly in the background. Lois must have turned on the stereo before she left, hoping the holiday music would lift Cricket's spirits, but it only made her feel worse. "All is calm, all is bright," sang the choir.

"All is calm—that's a joke, huh, girl?" Cricket murmured. Treasure paced the room. Maybe, Cricket thought, she wanted Dominic. Maybe if she let Treasure choose, the dog would go with him.

"You're just nervous 'cause I'm nervous, right?" Cricket asked.

Bending so close that tiny black whisps of fur curled against her lips, she whispered, "I can't lose you, Treasure. Not even for Dominic."

The rumble of a car motor made Cricket's stomach squeeze with fear. She leaped to her feet and ran to the window.

Silver dollar–sized snowflakes streaked through the beams of a car's headlights. For an instant she thought Dominic had come, but then she heard the familiar squeak as their garage door rolled open. Her mother was finally home.

"Mom, Mom, they're trying to take Treasure away from me! You've got to help!" Cricket cried as her mother came through the door.

"What? Cricket, give me a chance to take off my coat!"

"I can't—there might not be time! When Dominic saw Treasure he said she was his! He said he had papers and was coming back to get her and—"

"Wait a second, you're talking too fast. Sit down; let me get rid of a few things!"

Her mother dropped her leather briefcase, flung her coat over a chair, kicked off her shoes, then joined Cricket on the couch. She looked tired, as though some of her polish had worn off during the long day. Taking Cricket's hand, she asked, "Now what's this all about?"

"Dominic said Treasure is his dog. He wants her back—Mom, you can't let him take her!"

"Wait!" her mother said firmly. "How does he know that the dog is his? Did Treasure recognize him?"

Looking away, Cricket nodded. It still hurt to think of the way Treasure loved Dominic.

"Then you think Treasure is his dog?"

Cricket's head snapped back. "No! Maybe she was, once, but she's mine now. She *is* mine, right? I bought her!"

Her mother sighed deeply. She rubbed the tips of her fingers, painted bright cherry, into her pale forehead. "I don't know, Cricket. This is complicated."

"But you're a lawyer! You've got to fix it for

me!" She gripped her mother's arm tightly. "Dominic's dad is a policeman. What if he comes back with his gun?"

Her mother shook her head. "Don't be silly. Treasure's just a dog!"

Just a dog! Cricket thought fiercely. Just a dog? How could her mother say that? Treasure was her family!

"That dog," she said hotly, "is all I have. Dominic has two sisters and a mother that's always there. I don't. He can spare Treasure."

Stung, her mother cried, "Oh, Cricket! Be reasonable! Dominic must have loved Treasure, too. . . ."

"Not as much as I do!"

"But if the dog belonged to him . . ."

Cricket sprang to her feet, her eyes wide with fear. "I won't give her up—don't make me! I thought for sure you'd be on my side!" And then, even though she'd resolved not to, Cricket burst into tears. In an instant she felt her mother's arms encircle her, holding her tight. She smelled of stale perfume and office smoke. Patting her head as though she were a small puppy, her mother said softly, "Okay, honey, that's enough now. Stop crying. Technically, I don't think you'll have to give Treasure back."

"Really?" Cricket sobbed.

"I was trying to think of what was fair. If you want legal, well, that's another matter."

"All I want is Treasure," Cricket sniffed, rubbing her nose with the back of her hand.

"Don't do that, Cricket. Use a tissue. I know you want your dog, but honey, I want you to be really sure you know what you're doing. You and Dominic have spent a lot of time together lately. . . ."

"I don't care! It doesn't matter! He can't have my dog!"

Cricket took the Kleenex her mother held out to her and wiped under her eyes, then under her nose.

"Sit down." Her mother pulled her into the sofa cushions and leaned her cheek against the top of Cricket's head. "I want you to think about something, even if you don't want to. Dominic had Treasure first—" She held up her hand. "No, let me finish. Dominic probably raised her from a puppy. He was the one who fed her. He was the one who trained her."

Cricket felt her heart skip a beat.

"Now for your side. You bought Treasure from the pound. Legally, that makes Treasure yours."

"Can Dominic get her back?"

106

Her mother shook her head. "No. We paid the pound, and that's a contract."

Cricket sprang from the couch like a jack-in-the-box. The idea of losing Treasure had pressed on her, and suddenly she felt as light as a bubble.

"I knew it, I knew it!" she cried, twirling herself in joyful circles. "I hope he comes back! I hope he brings his dad! I'd just like to see the look on his face when we tell him!"

She grabbed Treasure's front paws and pulled her to her hind legs. Treasure stepped awkwardly around Cricket's sneakers, as though she too were dancing.

"Did you hear that, girl? We've got a contract. It doesn't matter what Dominic says. We'll always be together!"

14

"WHERE'S YOUR BOYFRIEND?" MELANIE SMIRKED.
"You haven't kissed up to Duminic all week. Are
you two still fighting over your dog?"

"He's *not* my boyfriend. He's not even my
friend," Cricket snapped. "Just drop it, Melanie."

"Sure, no problem."

"I don't want to talk about it, and I don't want
to talk about *him*!"

"I *said* okay!"

Melanie stood behind Cricket in the hot lunch
line. She pressed the edge of her tray into the
small of Cricket's back, pushing her forward. It
had been a week since Dominic discovered Trea-

sure, and in that whole time he hadn't talked to her once, not even when he passed out test papers. When he'd come to Cricket's desk, he'd spun her test so fast it skittered across her desk and landed on the floor. Cricket had turned to watch him carefully place the other kids' tests, score-side down, along the rest of the row.

"Did you see what Dominic had on today?" Melanie asked as Cricket plucked a carton of milk from the bin. "His shirt was red and blue, and his pants were *brown.* Can you believe it?"

"So?"

"So he must be blind. That boy needs dark glasses and a white cane!" Giggling, Melanie grabbed a fork and spoon.

Cricket slid her tray along the chrome countertop. A lunch worker scooped mashed potatoes, dropping them with a thud in a section of her tray.

"Maybe Santa will leave him some better clothes," Melanie went on as peas and then chicken and gravy plopped next to the potatoes. "You know, something from the Salvation Army bin!"

"I told you to shut up about Dominic!"

Melanie's eyes glittered as she spat, "I *knew* you were still in love with him!"

"I am *not!*"

109

"Then why are you defending him?"

Cricket turned slowly to stare down at Melanie. She was short, tiny, and thin-boned, like a bird. But she was mean as a cat.

"Dominic tried to steal Treasure from me. I hate him now, okay? He can dress like a bag lady for all I care. I just don't want to talk about him!"

Melanie was laughing, but it wasn't the kind of laugh that made Cricket feel happy. Chewing on the bottom of her lip, Cricket picked up her tray and headed for a table.

"Hey, Cricket, why don't you sit with us?" Melanie called after her.

Shrugging her shoulders, Cricket followed Melanie. She'd sat all alone since her fight with Dominic. Better the three of them than no one.

On the night Cricket talked to her mother, she'd waited for Dominic and his father to come. A few cars and trucks had crept down their road, inching along in the blinding snow, but the Falcone's blue truck never came.

It's because of the snowstorm, she'd thought. We'll have it out tomorrow at school.

But when Cricket found Dominic the next day, he was leaning against the school building, his hands deep in his pockets, his hair whipped by the wind into dark tufts. Several of the kids from the

Crackerbox houses huddled in a half circle around him.

Right then she'd meant to breeze past the other kids, look him right in the eye, and explain all about the law, but he'd stared at her with such anger that she'd just turned around and walked away.

"There she goes," Joey Jenkowitz had called after her. "A real rich witch."

"Yeah," another voice yelled. "Why doesn't your mummy just *buy* you another dog?"

"She'd rather have someone else's—that way she thinks it's more fun," shouted another.

Cricket had run off, her cheeks burning. Fine, she'd thought. If that was the way they wanted to be, fine. She had Treasure. Dominic could hate her for it, no problem. They would be enemies; in fact, that would be better. She'd yanked open the school door and run down the narrow hallway, polished in the night until it shone like glass. Darting into her homeroom, Cricket had run straight into Mrs. Chumley's soft middle.

"Uumph, Cricket, you're here early!"

"Mrs. Chumley," Cricket began, her mind racing, "I need to have my seat moved. Could I switch with someone?"

"Why?"

"Because . . . I . . . I can't see. I think I need glasses."

"Really?"

"Yes. Can I move up front?"

Mrs. Chumley had frowned, puzzled. She'd fingered a small plastic snowman pinned to her lapel and said, "By all means, Cricket. I had no idea you were having trouble. I'll help you move your desk."

The two of them pushed her desk down the side aisle, past the bulletin board decorated with paper snowflakes, Christmas trees, and menorahs made of gold foil.

"I put Joey near me for acting up," Mrs. Chumley had puffed as they pulled Joey's desk into Cricket's spot. "Let's see how he does here in the back. I know he'll be happy with the change."

When the rest of the kids filed in, Cricket had already been at her seat, studying. "Hey, rich witch, you're in my desk," Joey'd complained.

"You've been moved," Cricket told him coldly.

"Oooh, sucking up to the teacher. Fine by me—I'm out of here!"

And so the week had gone by, and with each passing day Cricket had grown more and more miserable. Now there were only six more days until Christmas break. Cricket sighed as she unwrapped her straw and jabbed it into her carton of milk.

"What ya thinking about?" Skye asked.

"Nothing."

"You know, Cricket, it never was a good thing the way you hung around with that Dominic. I mean, just look at him. What a geek!"

"Cricket told me she hates him now," Melanie said in a loud voice.

Skye laughed sharply. "Don't you just love his hair? I think his mom dropped a bowl on his head and then cut it."

"I bet she used pinking shears," Heather snickered.

Hurt bubbled in Cricket, hurt and anger at the whole stinking situation. If she hadn't been Dominic's friend, hadn't laughed with him and played games, she wouldn't have known what kind of friendship she was missing. But now, sitting next to Skye and Melanie and Heather, she knew. A sore, empty place ached inside her, and it was all Dominic's fault.

One by one, Cricket squashed her peas with her fork. If only he hadn't tried to take Treasure, everything would have been perfect. If only he'd talk to her! Surely he could understand that Treasure was really hers. She was going to tell him that

113

he could visit Treasure as often as he liked, but his dark eyes kept her away.

Cricket drew in a deep breath, then glanced from Melanie to Skye. Maybe they were right. Maybe Crackerbox and Pepperwood just couldn't mix.

Suddenly, someone bumped into her from behind.

"Excuuuuuse me. Did I touch her snottiness?" It was Joey again. His lips curled in an ugly sneer.

"He's too stupid to even talk to." Skye commanded, "Just ignore him."

"Did you all know that Cricket's got Dominic's dog?" Joey went on. "She can buy a million dogs, but she has to have someone else's. Makes her feel big."

"She got her dog from the pound," Melanie said defiantly. "That makes it hers."

"Oh, big deal. The pound. I'm so impressed."

"Leave it alone, Joey."

It was Dominic. Cricket's heart jumped at the sound of his voice. He stood right behind Joey, close enough for Cricket to touch.

"I'm just sick of these stuck-up rich girls," Joey shot back. "They think they own everything. They think they can do whatever they want."

"If we could do what we wanted, then we'd sure

as heck get rid of you," Skye said sweetly. "You're smelling up the whole school."

"Oh yeah?" Joey stuttered.

"Oh yeah," Melanie echoed sarcastically.

"Come on, forget it," Dominic cut in. "They'll always win 'cause their parents got money. They could steal anything, even somebody's dog, and it wouldn't matter."

Cricket turned so she could stare at him. "If you're talking about Treasure, you ought to know buying isn't the same as stealing. I paid forty dollars for her."

Dominic shook his head and snorted. Scarlet blotched his cheeks. "I paid one hundred and seventy-five dollars for Coty. Now you've got her. Sounds like stealing to me!"

"Well, if you cared so much why didn't you come back to get her?"

The table was suddenly quiet. Everyone around them seemed to stop, their forks suspended in midair, watching the two of them finally face off. How many kids were in on their fight? Cricket wondered.

"My dad wouldn't let me even try to get Coty back. He said it was stupid to fight someone who had a lawyer for a mother, 'cause lawyers don't care squat about what's right. All they want to do

115

is win. And they'd walk over anybody to do it."

Cricket didn't know what came over her then. She'd been angry before, but never like this. Dominic was trying to blame her mother! Before she could think, Cricket picked up some peas and threw them at Dominic. They bounced off his shirt like tiny rubber balls. "Just shut up, Dominic!"

Dominic glared at her, his eyes blazing.

Slowly, Cricket turned back to face the table. It was such a stupid thing to do! She had to get control of herself! She was just about to pick up her napkin when she felt a smack on the top of her head. A clump of mashed potatoes oozed down her forehead.

"Joey, you moron!" Skye shouted. Melanie grabbed her sweet roll and spun it like a frisbee over Cricket's head. Because they were standing behind her, Cricket couldn't tell whether it was Joey or Dominic who got hit, but one of them yelled, "Crud!"

"Too bad it didn't get stuck in your mouth!" Melanie smirked.

In a flash Joey reached over Cricket's shoulder, grabbed a handful of mashed potatoes and threw them at Melanie. They splattered across her face like lumpy glue.

116

"You *jerk!*" Melanie screamed. She scooped her own potatoes and threw them back.

"Food fight! Food fight!"

Green peas, chicken, mashed potatoes, even milk went flying, smacking, splattering onto their targets. Cricket grabbed fistfuls of her food and threw them in Dominic's direction. Nothing mattered but hitting him. Mashed potatoes squeezed underneath her fingernails; frosting stuck to her skin; pieces of meat whirled around her until it seemed as though they were all caught in a gigantic blender.

"Stop it every last one of you or you'll all be suspended!"

The voice of their principal pierced the confusion. Cricket let her fist drop slowly to her side.

"I want this entire table cleaned up in ten minutes. What a disgrace! Then you, Dominic, Joey, Skye, Heather, Melanie, and Cricket better scrub that slop off and march your behinds right into my office. *Move it!*"

15

"WELL," MR. HADSHAW DEMANDED, "WHAT IS THE meaning of that display in the cafeteria? Skye, Melanie, Heather, I'm surprised you girls would be involved in a food fight!"

"It wasn't our fault," Skye cried. "It was that jerk Dominic. . . ."

"No, it was that stupid Joey. . . ." Melanie shouted.

"It was not!" Joey shouted back. "You stuck-up—"

Mr. Hadshaw held up his hand. His brows came together as he barked, "No name-calling! Now let's just stop for a minute and think. What caused all of this?"

Cricket shifted uncomfortably. They all had to stand together in the principal's office, which meant she was only three feet away from Dominic. Looking at him from lowered lids, she noticed a spot of mashed peas drying behind his ear. She felt a twinge of satisfaction.

"Well," Skye began, "I guess the very first thing was the fight about the dog."

"Dog? What dog?"

"Cricket's dog."

"My dog!" Dominic exploded.

"No way!" Cricket shouted back. "Possession is nine-tenths of the law—"

"Hold it!" Mr. Hadshaw's voice sounded like the blast from a horn. "I didn't call you in here to witness another fight. Can anyone explain this in a calm and orderly way? Anybody?"

Stepping closer to Mr. Hadshaw's large wooden desk, Cricket took the lead.

"I bought a dog from the pound about six weeks ago. I named her Treasure. Now Dominic says that she's his dog and he's trying to take her from me!"

"She *is* my dog. I can prove it!"

"Now just hold on! I can only hear one of you at a time. Now Dominic, you say you can prove Treasure is your dog?"

Dominic crossed his arms over his chest. "Her name is Coty. I have her registration papers, but Cricket doesn't care. She's hiding behind her mother 'cause she's some hot-shot lawyer—"

"I am *not*!" Cricket blazed. "I don't need to hide behind anybody, 'cause I'm right. Ask Mr. Hadshaw, ask anyone in our class. They'd all say Treasure's mine!"

"All my friends think I'm the one who should keep Coty!" Dominic shot back.

"Your friends! You don't even *have* friends—"

"I'm his friend," Joey yelled.

"That's what I mean," Cricket retorted.

"Stop!" Mr. Hadshaw bellowed. The wheels on the bottom of his chair squeaked as he rolled it back and stood up. He smoothed his thin hair with the palm of his hand, then ran fingers down his lapels. Mr. Hadshaw always looked slightly rumpled to Cricket, sort of like the brown paper sacks the Crackerbox kids packed their lunches in. Now he looked hassled, too.

He leaned across the desk and rested his weight on his knuckles. "I've heard enough," he said. His brown tie dangled over his coffee cup, then landed on top of a half-eaten doughnut. Heather giggled.

"Melanie, Skye, Heather, Joey, you're excused. But if you ever throw food again, it better be into a trash can. Is that understood?"

"Yes, sir," they said meekly.

Mr. Hadshaw waited until the four of them left, then turned his eyes onto Cricket and Dominic.

"I'm going to make a couple of phone calls. In the meantime, I want you two to wait in the outer office until I'm done. If there is any chance you can work this problem out, now's the time to do it."

"No way," Dominic muttered.

Cricket just rolled her eyes at the ceiling.

"Suit yourself." Mr. Hadshaw pressed a button on an intercom.

"Yes?" a faraway-sounding voice asked.

"Ms. Tharp, I'd like you to bring in the information cards on Kristin Winslow and Dominic Falcone. Right now, please."

"Certainly," the voice answered.

Sweeping his arm toward the door, Mr. Hadshaw said, "Wait outside. Ms. Tharp will call you back in when I'm done."

Cricket marched out first, letting the door swing shut on Dominic's arm. She plopped herself in the first chair and pretended to look at a painting that hung next to the secretary's desk. The picture was of bright orange and yellow sunflowers.

Dominic sat in the chair farthest away from hers, with his back poker straight and his hands clenched tight. He looks like he swallowed a yardstick, Cricket thought smugly.

Click click click. Ms. Tharp's heels tapped daintily as she walked across the linoleum. Dominic ignored her and picked a scab on his left hand. His frown was so deep his eyebrows touched in the middle.

I'm missing math, and now I'll have work to take home. Darn him! She crossed and uncrossed her legs. *Bang!* A file drawer in the office slammed shut, and the sudden noise made her jump. Cricket heard Dominic snicker. Turning her back toward him, she watched Ms. Tharp ruffle through a filing cabinet, pull out some cards, then disappear into the principal's office.

In was suddenly very quiet. She could hear Mr. Hadshaw's muffled voice rise and fall. What was he doing in there? Cricket swung her foot back and forth like a seesaw.

She'd made it to the fifth grade without getting into trouble, and now she'd been here twice in four weeks! Biting the bottom of her lip, she sneaked another look at Dominic. If only she could ask him what he thought, but she couldn't. They were enemies now.

After what seemed like forever, the office door flew open and Ms. Tharp called them back inside. This time it was Dominic who raced ahead. Ms. Tharp held the door.

"I've just gotten off the phone with your parents," Mr. Hadshaw began. "First, let me say one thing. I could have suspended the six of you for that display in the cafeteria. But if you agree to my plan, and whatever decision is reached, well, that will be the end of it. Agreed?"

Cricket nodded, even though she didn't understand a word he said.

Mr. Hadshaw webbed his fingers together, then continued. "Now, about the dog. I don't like to treat a symptom of a problem, like the two of you throwing food, and ignore the cause. And in this case, the cause is the ownership of that animal."

Out of the corner of her eyes, Cricket saw Dominic stop fidgeting. He stood perfectly still.

"We live in a democracy. We are governed by laws. I think it's important to both understand our laws"—he paused for emphasis—"and obey them. Therefore, I will have your teacher pick

twelve students from the other fifth grade class to
be jurors. Dominic, Cricket, I want you to repre-
sent yourselves. You will each explain to the jury
why you feel you should be the one to keep the
dog. The jury will listen carefully, then decide
which of you is right."

Cricket felt her breath catch in her throat. Panic
welled inside her.

"Your parents have agreed with my idea. They
also agreed to honor the verdict, no matter which
way it goes. So, next Friday morning, come prepared. We're going to have a trial!"

16

"How could you do this to me? how could you?"

Her mother was sitting in a dark green leather chair, going through some notes from her office. Slowly, she removed her reading glasses, folded them, and placed them on the edge of her green blotter. She looked up at Cricket.

"I did what I thought was best. For everyone."

"You did what was best for Dominic! Not for me! I had Treasure, and now I might lose her. Why didn't you tell Mr. Hadshaw no? Why?"

Standing over her mother, Cricket noticed for the first time how old she looked. The skin under her eyes was puffy, tinged with blue, and there were deep creases Cricket had never seen before. Her mother pinched the bridge of her nose with her fingers.

"Listen to me," she said in a tired voice. "Mr. Hadshaw called Dominic's house first. It seems they are very upset over this whole thing. And to tell you the truth, I can understand why. It's been hard on Dominic to move out here, to make new friends, to adjust. It was a real blow to lose his dog—"

Although Cricket hadn't done it since she was three, she stamped her foot hard. The sound was muffled by the thick carpeting.

"Dominic, Dominic! Why don't you worry about *me!*"

"I *am!*" her mother said, her voice rising. "I think you will keep Treasure, and maybe Dominic can accept the loss when twelve classmates tell him that it's fair. Maybe then this ridiculous fighting will stop!"

Cricket felt her ears get hot. "But what if I lose? These are just dumb kids from my class, and Mr. Hadshaw said their decision is *final*! I hate Dominic! I hate this trial! It's wrong! *He's* wrong!"

Her mother reached out and took Cricket's hand. She squeezed it firmly.

126

"Honey, this time neither one of you is wrong. You each have a good case for keeping Treasure. But I *can* do this for you. I'll help you prepare your case. I'll teach you every trick in the book, and we'll go through every step together. Okay?"

Cricket stabbed her toe into the carpet, digging a small hole between the fibers.

"Okay, Cricket?"

Cricket's voice shook. "Okay."

"Oh, sweetheart." Her mother softened. "I know you're scared." She pulled her close, into creamy folds of ivory silk. Cricket's cheek rested against a double strand of pearls, cool and hard against her skin. Was it her mother's heart or her own that hammered like a rabbit's? Rubbing her hand across Cricket's back, her mother gently added, "You know, we can always get another dog."

"If someone tried to take me, would you say, 'Oh, well, I can always get another kid'?"

"That's not the same. You're my child, and I love you."

"Treasure's my dog," Cricket said, "and I love her. And Treasure loves me."

Her mother kissed the top of her head.

"She loves Dominic, too."

Cricket, tears blurring her eyes, whispered, "I know."

"Okay, let's do one final check," her mother said, surveying the cue cards and notebook set neatly on top of Cricket's vanity.

"You've got all your copies made?"

"Check."

"And your cue cards are in order? Did you number them?"

"Yeah. Now I need to figure out what to wear. I don't have a single thing in my whole entire closet!" Cricket said, resting her hand on her mother's arm.

"Ooohh, honey, your hands are cold. Calm down, sweetie, we'll find something. Hmmm." Her mother tapped her cheek with her index finger. "Let's see, it can't be anything frilly, or the jury might assume you're a silly little airhead. No pants, either. Give them the message that this case matters to you." She opened the louvered closet doors and said, "I think your navy wool skirt with the white blouse and navy bow will look sensible and matter-of-fact."

"Oh, Mom," she protested, "I look like a nun in that outfit."

"Trust me, Cricket. Let's see . . . navy shoes,

and"—she crossed to the dresser—"I think white panty hose will look better than navy panty hose. What do you think?" She looked up from the drawer and smiled at the expression on Cricket's face. "If it'll make you feel better, you can wear white earrings and a bracelet. Nuns don't wear jewelry."

"Will any of this really help? Will it let me keep Treasure?"

Shaking her head, her mother replied, "The most it will do is give you an edge."

As her mother crossed back and forth, busily piling the clothes on a chair, Cricket pulled her hair up into a knot on the top of her head. She tilted her face from side to side, studying herself in the vanity mirror. "What do you think?" she asked, frowning as deeply as she could. "Do I look more serious without hair?"

"You look positively dour. Still nervous?"

Cricket let her hair drop and nodded. Whenever she thought about the trial her stomach jumped into her throat.

"Just try not to think about it too much. Whichever way it goes, at least tomorrow is your last day before Christmas break." She rummaged through rows of shoes, muttering, "Where is that pair? Ahh, there it is!"

"Mom?"

"Hmmm?"

"Who do you think is going to win? Me or Dominic?"

Without a word, her mother placed Cricket's navy shoes underneath the vanity chair. The skirt, blouse, panty hose, fresh underwear, and jewelry were already draped over its back.

Cricket walked directly in front of her mother and repeated, "Who do you think, Mom?"

Her mother lightly touched the curve of Cricket's cheek, then smoothed a strand of hair from her daughter's upturned face. Finally, she murmured, "I really don't know."

That night, Cricket pulled Treasure to the top of her bed. She ran her hand through swirls of fur, fingering it into soft piles. The two of them had gone for a walk right before bed, and Treasure had zigzagged through the backyard, her nose either tunneling the snow or cutting through the air like a flag. Although she'd rubbed Treasure with a towel as hard as she could, her fur was still damp from the melted snow. For once it didn't matter. She held her close and burrowed her face into Treasure's neck, which smelled of woodsmoke and evergreen. "Your nose is cold," she

130

whispered. Treasure nuzzled under her chin.

"I never did paint your fingernails." She examined the long, light pink claws. "I always thought I'd do it. Maybe, if you're still here, I could paint them red and tie a great big bow around your neck for Christmas."

If you're still here. The words sliced through her. She went on in a husky voice, "I . . . this could be our last time together. I want you to know, if Dominic takes you away . . ."

Treasure's eyes looked at her, warm and brown. In a way, Cricket knew she was being silly, explaining things to a dog. But she'd always told Treasure everything, and she knew she'd have to tell her this. The words clutched in her throat as she said, "If he takes you away, I want you to know that . . . you've changed my life. I've never had anyone to wait for me, like when you stick your nose in the window and watch for me to come home. And, if things don't work out"—she took a deep, wavering breath—"I'm glad I had you, even for a little while." A tear ran down her cheek, dropping silently into Treasure's fur.

Treasure whined and pawed the comforter. She rolled to her back. The soft folds of her mouth hung open, revealing sharp white teeth.

Cricket stroked the feathery fur, then one by

one touched the freckles that dotted her dog's pink belly.

"The other part I haven't said to anybody, is . . ." She swallowed hard. "I . . . I miss Dominic. He hates me now, and I can't let him win, but . . . I miss him so much!"

Never before had she felt so much pain. It washed through her, crashing against her like a thundering wave. Treasure watched, bewildered.

"Come here, baby," she said, rubbing the tears away with the palms of her hand. "Don't worry, I won't cry anymore. As long as I have you."

Even though she wasn't supposed to, Cricket pulled Treasure under the covers and wrapped her arms tightly around her. She could feel Treasure's heart beating, and moments later felt her settle into slow, even breathing.

The outdoor Christmas lights winked through her window, flicking light, dark, then light across Treasure's sleeping face. She nestled her head next to Treasure's and stared at the ceiling. Finally, when the lights were turned off and the house had been locked for the night, Cricket slipped into a restless sleep.

17

"ATTENTION! ATTENTION EVERYONE!" MRS. CHUM-
ley cried. Noise filled the classroom. Metal legs
from twelve chairs scraped along the linoleum,
squeaking like chalk across the chalkboard. Everyone talked at once as they set up their homeroom
to look like a court of law.

"Quiet, children," Mrs. Chumley intoned as
she slipped into a black choir robe. "Now I want
the first jury row to use the kindergarten chairs.
That way the ones who sit behind can see."

Dominic paced at the back of the room. He'd
worn a blue linen suit, the color of a robin's egg,
with a matching tie and his everyday sneakers.

Little spikes of hair bristled at the back of his head. He must have had his hair cut for the occasion.

"Blue linen?" Skye whispered in Cricket's ear. "Doesn't he know you're only supposed to wear linen in the summer?" She shook her head and snickered.

Cricket studied the different points she'd carefully printed on her cue cards. The trial could go either way. She knew that. And now it was about to begin.

"Ladies and gentlemen of the jury, court is now in session. The case of Falcone versus Winslow. Please listen carefully to my instructions." Mrs. Chumley shifted, pulling folds of her choir robe free from underneath her behind.

"First of all, jurors, I want to thank you for taking time away from the other fifth grade class to serve as our jury. Remember, you are to decide this case on the facts. In other words, just because you're a boy doesn't mean you should vote for Dominic, and the same goes for you girls favoring Cricket. Your teacher Mr. Smith tells me you're very bright and honest young people. We're all counting on your careful attention to the details and trust that your verdict will be fair. Now then, let's turn the time over to Dominic for his opening remarks."

Dominic walked up to the front desk so that he was facing Mrs. Chumley. A piece of rolled-up notebook paper, twisted until it looked like paper rope, was clutched in his hand.

"Um," he began, his voice higher than Cricket had ever heard it, "I wanted to say about how unfair it is to . . ."

The door to the classroom opened with a bang.

"Excuse me, Mrs. Chumley, class," Mr. Hadshaw apologized. "I couldn't get away any earlier. Sorry for the interruption." Stuffing himself into one of the empty student desks, he commanded, "Go on with what you were saying, Dominic."

"I . . . uh . . . just wanted everyone to know I bought Coty first, and I will prove she's mine. Thanks. Thank you."

He looked shaken as he walked to his desk.

"Cricket?"

Cricket drew in a deep, cleansing breath, just the way her mother had told her to do, and exhaled slowly. She gathered her index cards together, tapped them against her desk, then stood up as straight and tall as she could. She walked directly in front of the jury and tried to look each and every kid in the eye.

"Members of the jury," she began as calmly as she could manage. "I first want to thank you all for being here. It means a lot to me to have people I trust making this important decision."

Suddenly Mrs. Chumley banged her gavel onto the desktop. "Joey Jenkowitz, if you stick your finger down your throat one more time you will leave this room. Understood?"

After the wave of laughter died down, Cricket went on. "What you are going to have to decide really isn't hard. Does the pound own the dogs that are left there or not?"

She walked down the row of chairs, then spun on her heel and walked back. With a quick glance at her notes she went on. "Maybe that seems like a tough question. It might be, if you or I had to decide. But we don't. We already have a law, and that law says that any dog left in the pound over five days belongs to the pound. Treasure was there for five days. The pound owned Treasure. I bought Treasure from the pound. Therefore"— she paused for emphasis—"Treasure is mine. Thank you."

Excitement flushed through her as she crossed

the floor to her seat. She'd done it! She'd smiled at them, talked to them, and they'd listened to her!

"Very good," Mrs. Chumley declared. "Dominic, would you like to call any witnesses?"

"Uh-huh. Yes. I would like Joey to come up."

Joey shuffled to the front of the room and plopped himself into a chair set beside Mrs. Chumley's desk. He slumped and shoved his hands into the pockets of his jeans.

"Sit up straight, Joey," Mrs. Chumley said.

As Joey pulled himself up, Dominic unrolled his paper. He looked at Joey.

"Do you remember the time I talked to you about my dog?"

"Yeah."

"Well, can you tell those guys, the jury, what I said?"

"You told me you left your dog with some man, and while you were gone it ran away and got lost."

Dominic crossed his arms and asked, "Do you remember what I told you I did after that?"

Joey shrugged his shoulders. "You said you put an ad in the newspaper and the nickel want ads, and you went around on your bike looking all over for your dog."

"Thanks, Joey. That's it."

"Do you have any questions, Cricket?" Mrs. Chumley asked.

Cricket placed her hands on the desk and slid back her chair. "Yes, I do. Joey, did Dominic ever tell you he went to the pound?"

"No. I think he called, though."

"Oh. Did you see him make the phone calls? Or did he just *tell* you he called?"

"He *told* me." Joey narrowed his eyes. "What do you want Coty for, anyway? Why don't you just go put a couple of dogs on your credit card?"

Mrs. Chumley banged her gavel and cried, "That's enough! Go sit down, Joey."

Cricket stole a glance at Dominic. He looked embarrassed. He unrolled his paper, studied it and said, "I'd like to show the kids the ads I put in the paper. Here, I xeroxed it. The one about Coty is circled. Is that okay?"

"You may hand them out."

As Dominic passed out the copies, he said "See, I did everything I could to find her. I rode all over looking for her and everything."

"Objection!"

Mrs. Chumley looked startled. Her eyes darted from Mr. Hadshaw to Cricket. "Why do you object to that?"

"Just because he put an ad in the paper doesn't mean he did everything to find her! He can't say that!"

Whipping around from the jury, Dominic spat, "Then I object too! Just because her mother is some hotshot lawyer . . ."

Bang bang bang went the gavel. "Order in the court! Order! Now stop that, you two. Stop it!"

The classroom buzzed. Heads rippled together from the back of the room to the front.

"Quiet, everyone!" Mr. Hadshaw's voice cut through the noise like a buzz saw. It became suddenly still. "Let's get on with this. Cricket, Dominic, act with a little dignity. Go on, Dominic. I believe it was your turn."

"I . . . uh . . . wanted to show them Coty's registration papers."

"All right. Is there anything else you'd like to say while you're doing that?"

Dominic shot a glance at Cricket. He squared his jaw. "Yes. I just wanted the jury to know that just because Cricket's got more money, that doesn't make her better for Coty."

Cricket shot up out of her chair. "Now I really object!"

"Sit down, Cricket. Dominic, you'd better confine your remarks to the case."

139

Reluctantly Cricket sat down. What if all the jurors were Crackerbox kids? These were students from Mr. Smith's class, and she really didn't know them. Maybe Dominic could get them to feel sorry for him. Maybe that was his edge.

She glanced at the jury. It seemed pretty evenly divided between Crackerbox kids and Pepperwood kids.

"Mrs. Chumley? Your honor?" Dominic said. "I have copies of Coty's registration papers. Can I give them out to the jury?"

"Then I'd like to hand out copies of my receipt from the pound plus a xeroxed copy of our check for forty dollars. . . ." Cricket interrupted. She grabbed a stack of papers and stood, eagerly approaching Mrs. Chumley's desk.

"Cricket, I know you're anxious, but you have to wait you turn!"

Dominic gave her a grim smile. Cricket's cheeks burned.

"Let's try to keep this in some sort of order. Dominic, do you have any more witnesses to call?"

"I do, your honor," he answered, turning to face Cricket. "I would like to call Cricket Winslow to the stand!"

18

"ME! HE CAN'T DO THAT!"

"Why not? I can too, can't I, Mrs. Chumley?"

Cricket's heart squeezed into her throat. How could Dominic call her to the stand? It felt as though someone had knocked her from behind, so that she was off balance. She hadn't expected him to do anything like that!

Mrs. Chumley slammed her gavel onto her desk top and shouted, "Quiet! The class will be dismissed to the library if you can't keep order any better than this. Now then," she said as the hubbub died down, "Dominic, you want to call Cricket to the stand. Well, I can't say I see anything wrong with that. I'm going to allow you to be called up. Come on, Cricket," she said, motioning her to the front, "take the stand."

Take a cleansing breath, Cricket told herself. Keep calm.

As she made her way to the chair, Cricket shot a look at the jury. They were watching her intently, like she was a bug in a glass jar. She slid into the seat and looked at Dominic.

"I was at your house about two weeks ago. Remember?" Dominic asked. Cricket nodded, wary.

"Now, you've got to tell the truth. . . ."

"I know that!"

"Okay. What happened when Coty saw me?"

A picture flashed in her mind, a picture of Treasure licking Dominic's face, bouncing against him and nuzzling his hair.

"What do you mean?"

"What do you mean what do I mean?"

That time the jury laughed. Cricket felt a rush of embarrassment.

Dominic walked directly in front of her, so close that she could have easily touched him. He leaned forward and asked again, "What did Coty do when she saw me?"

"She jumped on you."

"And?"

142

"And . . . I don't know, licked your face a little, I guess."

Dominic seemed to relax. He even gave her a tiny smile. Pleased, Cricket supposed, that she'd told the truth. Well, she wasn't done with him!

"The thing is," Cricket said out of turn, "Treasure jumps over anybody. She's not the least bit picky. We're trying to break her of the habit!"

The smile vanished.

"You saw the way she came to me! If you would have let her, Coty would have left your house right then and there!"

"Ha! Treasure licked the mailman more than she licked you!"

"I trained her from the time she was a little puppy!"

"Then I guess you're the one to blame for her bad manners!"

"Cricket! Dominic! This is a court of law!" Mrs. Chumley bellowed. Her gavel pounded against the desk. Dominic spun on his heel and walked until he faced a corner, away from the sixty-four eyes boring down on him. He stuck his fists deep into his pockets. The blue linen jacket stretched tight across his back, rising and falling with each jagged breath. What was he doing? Cricket wondered. She had her every move prepared and knew exactly where she was going. But Dominic just hung in that corner like a kid from the old nursery rhyme. All he needed was a dunce cap perched on top of his head. Cricket watched as he yanked one hand free and rubbed the back of his neck. He wasn't doing anything but standing there. Some of the kids on the jury began to whisper until Mrs. Chumley stared at them and shook her head. Cricket pulled on a hangnail.

Hurrrahugh! The sound was Mr. Hadshaw clearing his throat.

Finally Mrs. Chumley leaned across her desk and asked, "Dominic, do you have anything else to add?"

Slowly, he turned to face her.

"Yes, I . . . uh . . . had one more question."

"Then I think you'd better ask it."

"Okay. Cricket, do you think Coty was my dog?"

Her heart skipped a beat. "What?"

"I said," Dominic repeated, walking closer, "do you think Coty was my dog?"

For a second she felt scared, confused. Yes, Treasure was his dog, but how could she admit it? It was like saying Treasure belonged to him. Cricket dug her fingers into her palm. She heard

144

Mrs. Chumley shift forward in her seat. Taking a deep breath she said, "I think . . . I think Treasure was your dog."

The classroom buzzed. Dominic looked excited, as if he'd just smacked a ball over a fence.

"I think she *was* your dog." Cricket smiled. "But now she's mine."

"You can see from this paper that the pound owned Treasure at the time they sold her to me," Cricket went on. She was giving her final argument to the jury, and her insides flip-flopped like a bag full of fish. This was it. After she sat down, Dominic would say his last few words, and that would be that. The jury would leave the room, talk it over, and then decide what would happen to Treasure. And their decision would be final.

As she made one last pass in front of the jury, Cricket clasped her hands together as if she were praying. What was it her mother had said to do? Oh, yes: Stand in front of each jury member as though you were talking only to him or her. With each word, Cricket took a step sideways, her eyes resting on their faces as she spoke. "I love my dog." Step. "I'll give her . . ." Step. " . . . the best home ever. Please . . . *please!*" Step. "Let me keep

Treasure." Step. "It's up to all of you, now." Step. "Please, don't take my dog away." Step. "Thank you."

She floated back to her seat, numb. Dominic pulled himself to his feet and stood in front of the jury. One of his shoes was untied. He was sweating.

"I . . . um . . . I . . ." His voice sounded squeaky, as though the words had to be squeezed out of his throat. "See, when I was nine, I wanted a dog real bad. I wanted a springer spaniel. I begged my mom and dad to get me one, but they said we didn't have enough money." His face reddened, but he went on. "So I took a paper route to earn the money. I worked every morning before school, and on Saturdays I pulled weeds out of my neighbor's yard. It took me a whole year, but I made it. And when I had enough money, I bought Coty." He shifted from foot to foot. His eyes wandered the floor. "Then, when we came here, and I lost her . . ." He looked up and straightened. "I don't care about legal. I don't care what kind of papers Cricket gives you. I paid for Coty, I raised her, and she's mine. You should give her back to me." His voice dropped to a whisper. "That's all."

He walked back to his seat, his eyes still glued

to the floor. Mrs. Chumley stood and said, "Well now, you both did a very good job in presenting your cases. All of you jury members will go into Mr. Smith's classroom until you reach your decision, which," she said, glancing at her watch, "should hopefully take less than twenty minutes. That'll put us right in time for lunch." Shoving the choir robe sleeves up to her elbows, she walked around to the front of her desk and leaned against it. "There are just a few things I want you to remember. One . . ." She held up her index finger. "You have to be fair. Two . . ." She held up her middle finger. "Pay attention to the facts. And three," she said, holding up all three fingers, "follow the law. Okay, you're dismissed. The rest of the class will have a quiet time to read. Those of you who forgot to bring a book can get one from the back. Good luck!"

The jury stood and began to file out. A couple of the kids stretched as though they'd been sitting for hours instead of half an hour. Maybe they're bored, Cricket thought to herself. Maybe they were so bored they didn't listen and they'll give Treasure to Dominic. Her legs felt like sticks of wood as she walked back to her desk. She pulled out her copy of *What Happened in Hamelin* but her eyes couldn't focus. Words seemed to crawl on the page like thousands of tiny black ants. Why didn't they hurry?

Skye leaned over to Cricket and whispered, "Way to go, Cricket. You killed him! Dominic doesn't have a chance!"

"Thanks!" she whispered back.

"No talking!" said Mrs. Chumley.

Little bits of hope fizzed inside her. Was Skye right? Had she killed him? She thought of Dominic standing there, with his shoelaces resting against the floor, pleading for his Coty. She hadn't known he'd earned the money to buy his dog. She'd never had to earn anything in her life. All she had to do was ask her parents, and they'd buy it for her. Or send out Lois to get it. What would it be like to work and work, to save every penny until you had enough to buy what you wanted? Cricket shook her head. She didn't want to think about it.

Twenty minutes went by, then thirty. Mr. Hadshaw had left with the jury, and Mrs. Chumley was busy grading papers. What was taking so long? Her mother had told her of cases where the jury had to stay for three and four weeks before they made a decision. Maybe the class would have to stay the night. Maybe they'd even miss Christmas! Cricket pinched her arm. She was being stupid, silly. They'd have to make a decision soon. They were missing lunch.

"Mrs. Chumley," a boy named Daryl said, "we're getting hungry. How long is this going to take?"

"Well," Mrs. Chumley said, "I suppose . . ."

Suddenly the door opened. The twelve jurors filed in, each one looking at the other one's back. Her mother had told her if they looked at her it was a good sign, and if they looked at Dominic they'd probably go with him. What did it mean if they ignored them both?

"Oh!" Mrs. Chumley jumped. "You're back. Where's Mr. . . . oh, there you are, Mr. Hadshaw. Cricket, Dominic, why don't you both come back up to the front of the room?"

Never before had Cricket been so scared. It felt like the floor had turned to sand, as though each foot had to be dragged through a huge drift. She crossed her arms over her chest, hugging her sides. Dominic slid into his seat with a thud.

"I'd like to say a few words now," Mr. Hadshaw began. "Our justice system is the best in the world. Everyone has the chance to have his or her case heard by their peers. Today, Dominic and Cricket have had that privilege." He rubbed the side of his nose with his finger.

149

Hurry *up*! Get on with it! Cricket screamed inside her head.

"Thank you, students of the jury, for participating in this case. And although some might not agree with your decision, we all respect it. Let's give the jury a big hand of thanks!"

As the class applauded, Cricket bit into her lip so hard she tasted blood. She could see Dominic's jaw twitch.

"And now, will the foreman—excuse me, fore-*woman*—of the jury give Mrs. Chumley the verdict."

A girl named Rita walked up to Mrs. Chumley and handed her a scrap of paper. Mrs. Chumley opened it, read it, then handed it back to Rita.

"Rita, will you please read your verdict out loud in the case of Falcone versus Winslow?"

"Okay. Yes, your honor."

Rita turned to the class. She looked first at Dominic, then at Cricket.

"We, the members of the Woodland Elementary School jury, give the dog to . . ."

She opened the paper and read, "Cricket Winslow!"

Cricket fell back into her seat.

She'd won.

19

TREASURE LAY FLOPPED AT THE END OF THE BED, asleep. Cricket could tell her dog was on a dream hunt; paws twitched, her black nose flared, a muffled *mmmuft mmmuft* sound caught in her throat.

"Chasing space rabbits again?" Cricket whispered. She gently stroked the soft fur on Treasure's back. Treasure groaned and stretched, pushing her toes into little spikes.

"We won, girl. You're really truly mine. No one can take you away—you know that?" Treasure let out a deep, sleepy sigh. Cricket sighed, too.

She couldn't get the picture of Dominic out of

her mind. It had been like watching a beach ball with the plug pulled out. After Rita read the verdict, Dominic's body had slumped forward, his arms and legs hanging like four empty wind socks. Joey had rushed up to Dominic, while Skye and Heather and Melanie crowded around her.

"Way to go, Cricket!" Skye had chirped. "I knew they wouldn't give a great dog to a Crackerbox kid."

"Not to be rude, but did you see him standing there with his shoe untied?" Melanie had asked. "I mean, that must be the reason no one wears sneakers with a suit."

"You did it!" Heather announced, thumping her back. "The best person won!"

Skye moved closer and slid her arm around Cricket. Her earrings were shaped like Christmas trees, and Cricket knew they were made of real gold.

"You know," she'd said, "I hope you've learned something from all this. You'd never have had a problem if you'd stayed away from Crackerbox in the first place. If you hadn't let Dominic into your house, he'd never have known about Treasure."

"Crackerbox, Pepperwood, everything about that is so stupid," Cricket blazed. Shrugging

152

Skye's arm off, she'd said, "Dominic is just plain Dominic. A kid. And so are you."

The three of them had stared.

"I'd fight him again if it meant keeping Treasure," Cricket went on defiantly, "but he was a better friend than all of you. Oh, just forget it."

"No, we won't forget it," Skye had said, her voice ice. "You know, Cricket, we've given you a million chances, but you're hopeless."

Narrowing her eyes, Heather spat, "The only reason we've taken you back is because we thought we should stay together, but if you stick up for that Crackerbox loser, you'll never be one of us."

"Thanks," Cricket shot back. She'd looked each one of them in the eye, just the way she'd done with the jury. "That's the nicest thing you've ever said to me."

The three of them glared at her, then walked away. Right then Cricket realized that she'd crossed a line, one that couldn't be uncrossed any more. But worrying about who was Crackerbox and who was Pepperwood had stuck her with the most obnoxious girls in the school, and it was just plain dumb.

No matter what happens now, at least I have

Treasure, she'd thought. Just like before. Stealing a glance in Dominic's direction, Cricket checked to see if he'd heard their fight, but his seat was empty.

After lunch Ryan had passed out paper wreaths, the ones they'd worked on all week; Dominic's lay on his desk until Mrs. Chumley put it away. He'd missed the cherry punch and Christmas cookies and the carols sung by the first graders. He'd never come back. Maybe, she told herself now, as she lay in her bed with Treasure beside her, maybe he was never coming back.

I'm not going to think about it—I'm not going to think about Dominic. Everyone agreed with *me*! That should count for something! I don't care! I won! Her fist slammed the comforter fiercely. Treasure's coffee-colored eyes rolled open, then drifted shut again.

"Honey?" her mother called, knocking on the half-opened door. "I heard about your case—Lois told me. Congratulations!"

"Thanks."

In her charcoal power suit, her mother looked every inch the successful lawyer. Her hair was rolled into a sleek french twist; heavy silver earrings and a matching lapel pin reflected light like polished mirrors. She crossed the room and perched on the edge of the bed.

"So! Did you look 'em all in the eye? Were you nervous? How about the copies of the pound laws? Did you—"

Shrugging her shoulders, Cricket mumbled, "It went fine, Mom. Everything went fine."

"You don't seem too perky for a girl who just won her first case!"

Cricket shrugged again. "I am."

"How was Dominic?"

Cricket rubbed a spot on her pajama sleeve. "He was a dud."

"Oh?" Her mother's voice sounded high. "Why do you say that?"

"He just was. He didn't have anybody to coach him, the way I did. Mom?"

"Hmmm?"

"Do you—do you think that's why I won? Do you think I won because you helped me so much, or"—she took a deep breath—"did I win because I was right?"

Her mother reached out a finger to dot her nose, the way she had when Cricket was little. "You won because you were legally right. Twelve of your peers heard your case, and they chose to leave Treasure with you."

"But, Mom," Cricket asked, "is legally right the same thing as just plain right?"

Her mother leaned back onto the bed and kicked off her smoke-colored pumps. She shook her head gently, then looked Cricket directly in the eye.

"What do you think?"

Cricket sighed. "I don't know."

"Well," her mother said, propping herself on one elbow, "I don't know either. Sometimes the line gets pretty fuzzy."

"But you're a lawyer!"

"Yes, and in certain cases you can't point a finger and say, 'she's right, he's wrong!' "

Cricket straightened.

"I've never asked you this, but I want to know. I really want to know. If you were the only one deciding, who would you give Treasure to? Me, or Dominic?"

"Honey, you're my daughter—"

"If I weren't your kid."

"Well, the law says—"

"No. Forget all about legal. If you were a judge, and you wanted to just be fair, who would you give Treasure to?"

Her mother pushed herself up until she sat

looking at Cricket. "What's bothering you, sweetheart?"

"Nothing. Everything! I . . . when my name was read and I knew I'd won Treasure I was so sure! But, I keep thinking about the things Dominic said. He worked for over a whole year just to earn money to buy Treasure."

"And that made you feel bad?"

Cricket dropped her forehead into her hands. "Of course it made me feel bad. It made me feel terrible. But I don't want to give her back!"

"No, no, I don't blame you." Her mother's voice was calm, soothing.

"Then why do I feel so terrible when I should feel so good?"

"Slide down in bed so I can tuck you in. That's the girl. Look, honey," her mother said, pulling the eyelet comforter under her chin, "you're just finding out about something most of us learn later on down the road. There are times when black isn't so black and white isn't quite white."

Pleading, Cricket cried, "Tell me which is which."

"I can't."

"Why not?"

"Because I don't always know." She kissed the

top of Cricket's head and said, "It's late, and I don't want you worrying all night. You worked hard, the jury agreed with you, and you're going to keep your dog. I don't know what else to say except go to sleep and enjoy your victory. You've earned it." Rubbing Treasure's head, she said, "Good night to you, too, Trouble."

As her mother left, she flipped off the light and quietly shut the door behind her.

Treasure stretched, then curled against Cricket like a bear cub to its mother. She never moved from her spot for the rest of the night.

20

Snow blistered her face. This wasn't the fluffy snow that had fallen days before, but a sleety kind that whipped at her like tiny razor crystals. With one hand Cricket pulled her coat tighter to her chest. The other hand gripped a brand new leather leash, and at the end of the leash strained Treasure, eager to explore the new smells in this unknown neighborhood. Cricket bowed her head and allowed herself to be pulled further and further down the street.

"Slow down, girl!" she called out, but her voice seemed to blow back into her throat.

Even though it was only five o'clock, most of the

Crackerbox homes glowed with light. Christmas trees were wrapped in festive spirals of red, green, and white; Hanukkah lights blinked in windows. Rooftops glittered with icicles, and snowmen stood lopsided in a half-dozen yards.

"Treasure, *stop!*" Cricket cried, yanking on the leash. Treasure looked over her shoulder, annoyed, then sat her bottom gingerly in the snow.

"Sorry, girl," she panted, catching up to her dog at last. "We're almost there."

Snow stuck on Treasure's ears and clung to her eyelashes. She looked so beautiful, sitting there like a statue. Cricket knelt down. Freezing sleet bled through her jeans, biting her knees with cold. Cricket ignored it. She took Treasure's paw, searched her eyes, and said, "No matter what happens, never ever forget that I love you."

Soft strains of music from a nearby house floated around them. Cricket removed her mittens and stroked the wet fur with her bare hands.

From angels bending near the earth, to touch their harps of gold . . .

She hugged Treasure hard.

Peace on the earth, good will toward men, from heaven's all-gracious King . . .

Cricket stood. She grabbed the leash and said brusquely, "Well, let's get on with it."

160

Treasure wagged her tail and sprang to her feet.

The world in solemn stillness lay, to hear the angels sing.

Cricket stuffed the mittens into her pocket and kept walking. Two more houses, then one. And then . . . Cricket stopped on the sidewalk and looked at the front door of Dominic's house.

A large plastic wreath hung off center, and a plastic nativity scene, the kind that was lit from the inside, crowded a corner of the porch. She could smell woodsmoke. Puffs of smoke wafted from the Falcone chimney, only to be beaten by the snow into nothing.

They had a fire going. Maybe they have company, she told herself. After all, school was out just yesterday. Saturday is a big visiting day. . . .

A face peeked at her from the window; a tiny hand waved. It was Camille. Darn! She'd been seen! Panic raced through her. What was she doing here? She didn't have to do this! Cricket spun around, ready to run, then, slowly, deliberately, turned back.

"Come on, girl," she whispered. "Let's go."

Her boots made deep imprints as she walked up the sidewalk. Treasure's nose was high, sniffing

161

the air, until a smell from a bush caught her attention. She began to root at the smell, causing clumps of snow to fly from the evergreen branches.

"Treasure, heel!" she commanded. Treasure ignored her. "Heel!" she cried again.

Suddenly the front door flew open and Dominic stood, framed by a halo of light, glaring at her.

"What do *you* want?"

Cricket's throat felt so tight she couldn't speak.

"What do you *want*?" he repeated.

"Here," she said at last. She held the end of Treasure's leash toward him.

"What's that for?" Dominic took a step forward, his arms crossed stiffly in front of his chest. His cheeks, hair, and shirt were dusted with flour, his knuckles crusted with some sort of dough. His feet were bare. "If you're trying to . . ."

"I . . . want to do the right thing." Cricket swallowed hard, then held out the leash again.

Dominic's arms dropped to his side. He stepped onto the porch, hopped from foot to foot, and said, "Coty?"

At the sound of his voice, Treasure stopped rooting the snow. The leash snapped out of

162

Cricket's hand as Treasure lunged, barking, whimpering, into Dominic's arms.

"Mom, it's *Coty*!" Camille screamed from inside the house.

Cricket hurried to where Dominic and Treasure were standing. Hands shaking, she reached into her pocket and pulled out a small, brightly wrapped package. "This is for Treasure," she said. "On Christmas morning, tell her . . . tell her it's from me."

Dominic's eyes widened. "Cricket . . ."

Her hand shot up as she cried, "No!"

The leash lay coiled on the cement porch. She picked up the end of it and threw it at him, then ran down the walkway as fast as she could.

"What's going on?" she heard Mrs. Falcone call out. "Coty, what are you doing here? Oh, my goodness, where's Cricket? Nicky, isn't this wonderful? Get Cricket to come back. Hello, Coty darling!"

She couldn't stop running. Run run run, she told herself. Don't look back. The cold air felt like ice in her lungs; her boots clomped, heavy. Run, past the house with the music, past the snowmen, past the lights and the evergreen trees. The snow was letting up, with just a fine drizzle melting against her hot cheeks. Run, don't look back, just run. She stopped at the end of the street and leaned, panting, against a telephone pole. And then Cricket did look back. She saw the shadowed outline of Dominic, holding his dog, standing barefoot in the snow.

"Good-bye, Coty," she choked. Turning the corner, Cricket walked away.

21

"CRICKET, THIS IS DOMINIC. I JUST WANTED TO say . . . I wanted to say . . . thanks."

The receiver felt cold in her hand. She could hear Treasure yapping in the background, and laughter. That must be Camille, playing some sort of game with the dog. Maybe it was tug-of-war. Maybe Camille was holding a bone in the air, and Treasure was jumping like a jumping bean, trying to grab it with her sharp white teeth. Cricket shook her head and tried to erase the picture from her mind. Treasure wasn't Treasure anymore. Treasure was Coty.

"Cricket? Are you there?"

165

"Yes."

"Well, aren't you going to say anything?"

"You're welcome."

The line fell silent.

What was she supposed to say to him? Don't worry, I'm not sad anymore? Because it wasn't true. When she'd arrived home, half-frozen and crying, both her parents had been at the door waiting.

"The Falcones called us," her mother had said, pulling off Cricket's soggy coat and boots. "Why didn't you say something? Are you okay?"

Her father, already armed with a red terry cloth towel, rubbed her hair furiously. "I'm proud of you for making a hard decision. What you did took guts. If you'd like to . . ." He'd shot a glance at her mother, then continued, "I'll take you to a pet shop right now, and we can get another . . ."

"No!" Even Cricket had been surprised by the vehemence in her voice. "I don't want another dog. There's only one Treasure."

"It's all right. We understand," her father said gently.

They'd hugged her, the two of them with Cricket squeezed in the middle. "You did the right thing," they'd murmured, "the right thing."

The right thing. They'd both said it. But if what

166

she did was so right, why did she still hurt so much?

Dominic's sigh came through the telephone to cut into her thoughts. "Coty's really happy to be home, Cricket. She really is. But I think she misses you."

Cricket's voice cracked. "I . . . I miss her too."

"Would you like to come over and be with her? Everyone here'd like to see you. My mom would, and Camille and . . . me."

A tear plopped into the receiver. Cricket quickly wiped it away with the palm of her hand. Don't cry, she told herself fiercely. Don't be such a baby!

"Are you still there?"

"I'm here. Thanks for asking, but I can't 'til after Christmas. My grandparents are coming, and I'm supposed to stay at home and be with them." That was an excuse. The truth was she didn't feel ready to see Dominic and Treasure together. She rubbed her nose on the edge of her sleeve, swallowed, and asked, "What makes you think Trea—Coty, misses me?"

"She looks out the window a lot. And she whines. You know what, Cricket? It's going to take me a long time to unspoil her. The very first thing she did was jump on my bed. Mom's having a royal fit, but, this time, I think Coty's going to win."

"She slept with me every night." Cricket took a deep breath and went on, "Oh, I forgot to tell you, she gets a vitamin every morning. The only way I could ever get her to take it was to hide the pill in ice cream."

"Okay."

"And you should watch and make sure no food's left around. She'll steal anything."

Dominic laughed an awkward laugh. "Yeah, Coty's been a thief from the time she was a puppy."

"Oh. I guess you'd know, then."

There was a pause. Dominic cleared his throat. "You know what? Coty's only been here three hours, and she already snitched candy canes off the Christmas tree."

"We used to call her Trouble instead of Treasure."

Dominic laughed again. "One time she took my dad's slipper from under his bed and dropped it into her water dish."

"Really? She did that here, too! Only it was my mom's slipper-socks, and I wondered what the heck that was floating in her water."

"Did she ever blow bubbles for you?"

168

"Blow bubbles?"

"Yeah." Dominic chuckled. "I've seen her stick her nose in a toilet or a puddle or whatever, and then, pretty soon, all these bubbles start coming up. I swear I've seen her do it! I thought maybe she'd end up on that Stupid Pet Tricks show."

"Blowing bubbles? Well, that's Treasure, all right. I mean, Coty."

"Yeah," Dominic said softly, "it sure is."

Funny, Cricket thought to herself. Part of her ached when she talked about Treasure, but at the same time, a part of her felt better. Dominic understood her love for that dog better than anyone in the whole world. He understood, Cricket realized, because he loved Treasure too. She could feel the hurt inside lighten just a little. If she couldn't keep Treasure, at least she could talk about her. And probably, sometime, she could visit. It wasn't as if Treasure were gone forever!

There was a pause. Dominic's breath made puffing sounds over the phone. *Whewwww mmmuft whewww mmmuft.* He coughed. Cricket scratched her leg and waited. How long was this supposed to go on, she wondered. What else was there to say?

"Well," Cricket said, finally breaking the silence. "Thanks for calling. . . ."

"Wait! Don't go yet."

"You already said thanks. . . ."

"I know. But, see, I wanted to tell you something else."

"Okay." Cricket stretched and unstretched the telephone cord. "What is it?"

She could hear Dominic fumble with the receiver, and a muffled, "Just a minute, I'll be right there. Go away, Camille!" And then, louder, "Sorry, Cricket. I guess my dad needs the phone. Listen, the thing I wanted to say was . . . well, the thing is . . ."

"What?"

"Well, what you did today, giving Coty back, I know you didn't have to do it. Your folks didn't make you, right?"

"No. It was my idea. I think they were glad."

"Really?" Dominic sounded relieved. "That's good. But, I just want to say to you that . . . I'm sorry."

"I already told you it's okay. Treasure . . ."

"No," Dominic broke in, "not about Treasure. I'm sorry . . . that I wasn't as good a friend to you as you were to me."

Cricket was quiet, stunned.

"I mean, when things didn't go my way, I couldn't get past it. But you—you came through.

170

You're a real friend, Cricket. The best friend I ever had." A moment later he asked, "Are you still there?"

"I'm here," Cricket said. "Thanks, Dominic. Thanks a lot."

"Okay, I'm coming!" he yelled. He paused, then said, "I've got to go."

She bit her lip. "Merry Christmas, Dominic."

"Merry Christmas, Cricket."

When she hung up the phone, Cricket caught sight of her reflection in the hallway mirror. She was doing something she'd thought she'd never ever do again as long as she lived. Cricket saw that she was smiling.

22

"Here, sweetie, open this one. you're grow-ing so much I'm not sure it's going to fit!"

One by one Cricket unwrapped the presents her parents had stacked underneath their Christmas tree. Piles of clothing, two Madame Alexander storybook dolls, Nintendo, a microscope, and a pair of skis lay neatly to one side. A large box wrapped in blue and silver foil was the last gift she had to open. Yellow flames blazed merrily in the fireplace, seeming to flicker in time to the music playing softly in the background.

"I hope you like this," her mother said, smiling.

"Your father bought it in Germany, before, well . . ."

"What is it?" Cricket felt a rush of excitement as she tore the foil from the box.

"There's a store there that has every kind of gizmo you can imagine," her father said. "Trains with real smoke, and dolls bigger than you. When I saw this little guy, I said, 'I bet my Cricket would like you.' I hope you do."

Cricket pried the lid off the box and pulled fistfuls of tissue paper from inside. Swirls of cream-colored fur appeared. Carefully, she lifted a stuffed Pekingese dog from the box. Two brown glass eyes stared above a shiny plastic nose. "Like I said, I got it before—" he began.

"I love it," Cricket broke in. "Thanks Mom, thanks Dad." Placing the dog carefully on top of the clothes, she studied the animal. Its fur was long and silky, the kind you could comb, and its collar had a tiny gold license stamped with a red heart.

"You said you didn't want a real puppy. . ." His voice trailed off.

"No, not yet." She paused, then asked, "Can I go for a walk?"

"Now? But we haven't had breakfast," her

173

mother protested. "I've got special sausage, and strawberries, and fresh-squeezed orange juice. . . ."

"Just for a little while?"

Exchanging glances, her mother and father nodded. "Okay, but dress warmly. It snowed last night, and it's cold!"

Cricket grabbed the stuffed animal, then ran up the spiral staircase to her room. Placing the dog in the center of her pillow, she stepped back and stared at it.

"I bet you don't blow bubbles, do you?" she asked softly. The dog stared back, its glass eyes blank. Turning quickly, Cricket went to her closet and pulled a coral ski suit from a padded hanger.

Moments later, she called, "See ya, Mom, Dad." The door banged shut behind her as she stepped into the crisp air. Ice crystals sparkled in the sunlight, crunching beneath her boots like spun sugar.

Cricket headed toward the creek bed. She needed a place to think. Alone.

She picked her way through the brush until she found a sitting rock. Mounds of snow softened all the rocks to make them look like the backs of large white turtles. Idly, she plucked a branch from a bush and dug a tiny hole.

It was quiet. As she tunneled the stick deeper, Cricket pictured the stuffed Pekingese dog lying on her bed. A toy. All I've got now is a toy.

I could have had a puppy, she told herself. A real, live puppy. It would have been all mine, only I'm not sure I want one. She chewed the edge of her lip. But will I ever? There'll never be another Treasure.

Cricket squinted at the sun. The storm had washed the sky a clear, piercing blue, and the bare branches of the trees etched against it like black lace.

Suddenly, a sound cut through the stillness.

Arp! Arp! Arp arp arp!

Cricket sprang from the rock and looked around wildly.

"Treasure? Treasure girl!"

A black-and-white blur streaked through the trees, kicking up a spray as it raced headlong toward her. Cricket's heart skipped a beat. It was Treasure! Behind Treasure Dominic struggled knee-deep through a drift.

"Oomph!" Cricket cried as Treasure barreled into her, knocking her onto her bottom. "Get off me, you crazy dog. Stop, uck, dog kisses." She laughed and rolled as Treasure jumped again and again, nuzzling her neck with her wet black nose.

"Help, Dominic! Treasure, down! Oh, I love you! *Help!*"

"Merry Christmas, Cricket!" Dominic puffed, finally reaching her. "We came for a surprise visit. Coty, get off of Cricket. *Now!*"

Sheepishly, Coty left Cricket and ran to Dominic. She jumped on him, then raced back to where Cricket stood. Reaching down to pull her close, Cricket whispered, "I missed you, baby." She rubbed behind Treasure's ears, then cradled her head between her hands. Kissing the smooth spot between the dog's eyes, Cricket breathed the wonderful, wet smell of her dog.

Dominic stood watching. His skin was raw from the cold; his eyes looked bright.

"You know, when I go through these woods it's just a ten-minute walk to your house. I came out on Kelly Street, then cut over to Sterling Drive. I'll show you the way if you want."

Nodding, Cricket kept her eyes on Treasure.

"I hope we didn't come over too soon," he went on. "I called first, and your mom said it was okay. She told me you were out here."

Dominic had on a new aviator jacket, the kind with different patches splashed across the front. He tugged at the fingers of his matching gloves.

"You know, first thing this morning I could tell

Coty was dying to see you. She ripped apart that package of chew bones you got her, and then she stuck her nose at the door and started scratching like crazy. My dad said, 'Why don't you take her over to Cricket's house? I bet that's the nicest Christmas present Coty could have.' "

"I'm glad you came," Cricket murmured. She glanced at Dominic, then peered at the new tag dangling from Treasure's collar. Engraved across its center was the name COTY.

Dominic asked, "Did you get lots of good stuff?"

"Um-hmmm," she answered, her voice husky. "How about you?"

"Mostly clothes." He wrinkled his nose, then added, "I got a sled, though. I thought maybe later on today, we could try it out?"

"Sounds fun." She pulled her eyes from Treasure and looked at Dominic. He seemed so intent, so eager to see if she was happy, that she couldn't help but smile. "I got Nintendo. If you'd want, we could play a game."

Grinning broadly, Dominic nodded his head yes. "Hey, Cricket, watch this." He packed a small ball of snow in his hands and said, "We didn't have snow in Florida, so Coty really freaks out in this stuff. Look at what she does." He tossed the snowball, long and high, and called out, "Get it, Coty!"

The dog barked furiously, running as fast as she could until the snowball landed and disappeared into a drift. She spun in circles, searching, then jumped on a spot and began to dig.

"Trying to find a snowball in a bunch of snow is kinda dumb, Coty." Dominic laughed.

"She is not dumb; it's just new. Here Coty, show Dominic how smart you are. Fetch!" Cricket rolled a handful of snow right past Coty's nose like a bowling ball. Coty sprang on it, chewing until tiny ice chips flew from her mouth. When the last bit was gone she cocked her head in surprise. A little triangle of snow perched on the end of her nose.

"See? I told ya," he said, shaking his head. "Dumb dumb dumb."

Cricket began to giggle. "She is not—this isn't a good test." Scooping up another handful, Cricket flung it before Dominic had a chance to duck. It landed on his forehead, where it stuck to his hair and eyebrows.

"Okay! Watch out, Cricket!"

Squealing, Cricket ran three steps before she felt a ball smack her in the center of her back. She ducked behind a tree and returned fire, while

178

Coty spun and jumped like a marionette.

The air rang with laughter and barking as the three of them waged a snowy battle. Finally, Dominic held his hands over his head and yelled "Truce! I can't take any more! Coty keeps eating my snowballs, and she lets yours go!"

"I told you she was smart!"

"Naw, it's just that girls stick together." He brushed crystals from his hair and smiled so deeply that the corners of his eyes crinkled. "Hey, I've got a riddle. I made it up myself. Want to hear?"

"Sure."

"Okay. What has four arms, four legs, four ears, and four eyes, but it doesn't wear glasses and it isn't a bug?"

"What?" Cricket asked, making a face. "Are you sure this has an answer?"

"Yep! Give up?"

Cricket shrugged her shoulders and nodded.

"It's the people that love Coty Treasure Falcone. You and me."

Cricket reached down and hugged Coty tightly, then looked at Dominic's smiling face. He was right. The riddle had an answer, after all.

ALANE FERGUSON'S first published story is a picture book, *That New Pet!*, illustrated by Catherine Stock. Her second is YA fiction, a mystery called *Show Me the Evidence. VOYA* noted the mystery's appeal to "fans of Lois Duncan and Joan Nixon." And *School Library Journal* called it "chilling yet believable."

Cricket and the Crackerbox Kid is Alane Ferguson's first story for middle-grade readers.

The author lives with her family (daughters Kristin and Kathy, son Danny, and husband Ron) in Sandy, Utah,